GETTING Over HIM

Bonus Novella - Arianna's pov

CATHERINE EDWARD

Getting Over Him

This book is a work of fiction. Any similarities to real people, places, or events are not intentional and are purely the result of coincidence. The characters, places, and events in this story are fictional.

Cover art and design by June's Designs

Publisher: Self-published by Catherine Edward

Contents

In the loving memory of my father Mr. Edward.
To my mom, who always supports me in everything I do. To my fellow author and friend Rachelle Mills. To all my beloved readers for supporting me through thick and thin.

Chapter 1

"**H**ere comes the bride and groom to be!"

The excited voice on the speaker and the cinematic music in the background didn't evoke happiness in me. In fact, it added more fuel to my mental agony. My grip tightened around the glass of champagne, and I watched the bubbles settle down––tempting. When the waiter passed by, I swapped it for a glass of water. A deep breath expanded my lungs. Tonight, I had to be in control of my emotions.

The engaged couple descended the decorated stairs, hand in hand and with face-splitting grins. She looked gorgeous in her custom-made gown. Midnight blue suited her well. He wore a matching suit, looking handsome as ever.

I watched as his hand came around my sister's waist. He laughed at something she said, his eyes crinkling with amusement. How could he smile with so much ease? Pain spread across my chest, and I blinked away my tears.

What made it harder was watching *her* with him. Why couldn't it be someone else? Watching her was like looking at myself in the mirror. Alana, my twin, threw her head back, laughing. I could tell it wasn't genuine. Her blonde curls bounced over her shoulders.

The speaker boomed again. The voice of the party organizer was distant, and the surroundings faded. All I could see was them as they posed for the photos—pressing cheek to cheek, laughing and hugging. My eyes watered again when Brian dipped her, pecking her lips. The kiss garnered a round of applause.

Too dramatic? Yeah.

They announced the wedding date to the press and the guests. Brian and Alana would be married in three weeks. Their friends cheered around us. Our dad was full of praise for the young couple, especially the groom. He went on and on about how fortunate he was.

And here I was, wallowing and withering in my misery. *How am I supposed to rejoice when I know it should've been me sitting beside him? What did I ever do to deserve this?*

Am I not good?

No. He would've chosen me if I were good.

It was their engagement party. It should've been mine. *Ours.*

Both the Swanson and Schultz families beamed with pride and joy as they posed for photos. The news would make the headlines of tomorrow's business magazines. After all, this brought together two of the most influential business ventures in Linnesse.

Dinner was announced, and I moved robotically. The enormous banquet hall was another reason I never felt like I belonged here. When they built this mansion, they constructed a hall large enough to accommodate a hundred people when they hosted parties like this. And there was a party at least once every other month.

The people in my parents' elite circle loved these gatherings. They celebrated everything and anything.

Seeing my name beside one of her friends at the main table, I couldn't help but scoff. They didn't care to include me in any of their photos, but I had a seat at the main table. It could be the party planner.

They didn't know how things worked here. Why did I even bother to attend this?

My breath hitched at the sound of more cheers when they came in. His hand stayed on her lower back, and he pulled the chair for her to sit. I felt a pang in my heart. The simple action reminded me of the times he'd done the same thing when we dated. It warmed my heart, and I thought how sweet he was.

Brian's gaze never strayed from her face. He looked at her with so much adoration. I recalled how those same green eyes used to look at me like that once. They now twinkled with joy in contrast to the pain in mine. They appeared to be so much in love. He kept touching her. *How did this happen?* I took a deep breath and stared down at my plate, trying to hold in my tears. Even the food was to her liking. The Alfredo sauce was too cheesy for my taste. Honestly, I preferred plain pasta over this any day.

Her bridesmaids were laughing and chatting in high-pitched tones. *I am not one of them.* She didn't ask me, and no one ever asked why I wasn't on the list.

My throat clogged, and I forced my eyes down to not look at them and succeeded for a whole minute. However, my gaze had different plans because it went to the engaged couple again. My heart broke into a million pieces when he kissed her sparkling ring. *It's too much.*

My gaze locked with Brian's for a brief moment, and he turned to my sister casually, ignoring me.

"Excuse me." I stood to leave, and all eyes turned to me for a second. Not that they cared. After all, I was not their precious child. *It's always her.* Who'd choose a rebellious kid over a Disney princess, anyway?

The table was filled with laughter as I tried to escape with the little dignity I had left. No one tried to stop me as I rushed out of the crowded banquet hall.

Clumsy feet stumbled over the stairs, and I steadied myself. No one was here. Loud chatters echoed from the dining room below as I approached my sanctuary. Did he not feel any remorse for leading me on like that? I choked on my tears, locking the door behind me. Loud sobs broke out of my chest as if they'd waited for me to be alone. My knees gave up.

The day I met Brian was still fresh in my memory. It was a rough day, and I had just another incident with my sister's friends. I was running to my car when I stumbled upon a stranger with sparkling green eyes. The black t-shirt he wore hugged his chiseled body like a second skin.

There was something about his smile. Yes, that was what drew me in. I couldn't look away when his face lit up like a Christmas tree. Damn, those dimples. I could fall over and over again gazing at them, and I wouldn't mind.

Who knew it'd lead to my downfall?

I'd thought about my short-lived relationship with Brian too many times to count. Did I misunderstand his polite gesture? I did not misinterpret his attention. The words were clear. "Arianna, will you go out with me tonight?" Those were his words.

It wasn't her name he spoke. It was mine. What changed?

I'd never know. It looked like five months wasn't enough to understand a person. In the end, the time we spent together didn't matter. She was all that mattered to him. A perfect wife for his socialite life.

All those times we spent together, he never uttered her name, except for one day when I finally realized I had no place in his heart. I breathed through my mouth as the pain became unbearable. What could I do to take this pain away? I couldn't breathe and wanted to scream my lungs out.

My thoughts were in disarray. I couldn't focus on one thing. I was a mess. His laugh, soft touch, his eyes occupied my mind. Did he know how I felt when he got on one knee? For her. Two months ago, when my parents hosted that masquerade party, I didn't know I was in for a surprise. The kind that turned one's life upside down.

My thoughts pulled me back to the day my life came apart.

I was excited to meet Brian after his longest business trip. It was hard to miss his tall and handsome figure in the crowd. I spotted him with his sister, Kaylee.

Accepting one of the random dance requests, I stepped onto the dance floor. The lights glittered around us, filling me with an unknown joy.

While I wasn't fond of my parents' themed parties, being in the same place as Brian made it magical. The mask I wore covered my face, and I was curious to find out if Brian would recognize me. Perhaps we could get away from the crowd.

The eighties music filled the air as the floor lit up with multi-colored lights. My legs moved in rhythm as I watched Brian share the dance floor with Kaylee.

Dancing around, I slowly made my way toward them, wondering if he was looking for me. He acted as if he was in no hurry while he talked with Kaylee. Maybe it's because his family is here, *I told myself.* They weren't fond of me.

Brian always kept his distance from me in the presence of his parents. That didn't sit well with me. I did my best to win them over, but it wasn't my fault they didn't see me for what I was. I longed to be by his side, for him to make our relationship public. When I found out he was a Schultz, the knowledge wasn't pleasant since his mom had disliked me from childhood. Alana was her favorite.

Debating whether I should just cut in, I decided against it, seeing his mom approaching them. As time went on, I went to take a seat at the table, looking around at the guests. Then I noticed my sister, Alana, making her way toward Brian. His mother hugged her, chatting excitedly.

Foreboding set in the pit of my stomach as their eyes met. Something changed. My eyes didn't want to believe what they were seeing. The change in Brian's attitude was too obvious. When their dance began, Brian's hands were all over her body. The sound of my heart became too much for my own ears.

No. Just stay calm. It's just a dance.

But was it? He never looked at her that way before. Brian had met her twice, and he knew how I felt about her.

Keep calm, Arianna. You're just jealous.

However, deep down, I knew my worst fear was becoming a reality.

Wobbling on my legs, I rushed to the bathroom. My dress was suddenly choking the life out of me. Peeling off the velvet mini dress, I climbed into the cold shower, feeling numb when the water hit my body. All I could see and feel were Brian and Alana in each other's arms.

My life had become a living hell after their engagement. Brian didn't even have the decency to break up with me before proposing to my sister. Alana—she was a lost cause.

Despite us being twins, we were anything but similar. While she was the good one, I turned out to be the bad one. We were opposites then and grew apart. Our socialite parents never had time for us.

I knew why Brian chose her. Alana went on to become a business graduate, while I, the rebellious runt of the family, chose journalism, much to their chagrin. They weren't pleased because they wanted me to follow in their footsteps. An involuntary shiver ran through me, and I looked down to notice my pruned skin.

The conversation aftermath of their engagement came at me with full force.

"Why did you do it? You bastard, you led me on and made me believe we were a real thing. How could you do this?"

"I don't know what you're talking about, Arianna. I've always loved your sister." Brian's act of innocence stirred my anger.

"Liar! Why take me on a date, then? Why would you kiss me?"

"I kissed you because I thought you were Alana. Nothing more." His voice held no remorse as he spoke. In my peripheral vision, I saw a shadow, and my spine stiffened. Even without looking, I could tell who it was.

"You knew exactly who I was. Stop this nonsense now."

Brian exhaled as his eyes locked with mine. The pale green irises held no emotion. "That was before I met her."

I stiffened at his words. "You didn't even have the decency to break up with me before proposing to my sister."

"I hate to break it to you, Arianna, but we were never a thing."

I ground my teeth and balled my fists. The shadow—Alana—stood unmoving in her spot. Knowing her, she probably had a hand in this too.

"Alana was the girl I was supposed to meet that day. Meeting you was an accident. Look, I thought we were good. But things changed."

I felt used. How did I not see this?

Just as I opened my mouth to respond, Alana intervened. "He doesn't have to answer all your questions. If you are done talking with my fiancé, we're heading to bed."

"I won't cry again," I mumbled as I dried myself. It hurt. Crying didn't make it feel any better. It didn't take away the pain. I had to move on. I had to get out of this wretched place that had been my home for years. Except it never felt like home. *It never will.*

Why did I have to run? Why couldn't I stay and fight it? But wasn't running the first thing that came into everyone's mind? To run away and hide from all the problems.

Looking at the mirror, I barely recognized the woman staring back. She didn't sport that confident, flirty smile every time she got ready for a date. This wasn't the woman who spent hours straightening her unruly hair and setting it with hairspray.

This one was broken with red, puffy eyes and a runny nose. There was nothing sexy about this look. The dark circles beneath her eyes were more prominent, and the hazel in them once twinkled with mischief, now appeared hollow. The girl who once thought crying was for the weak now did nothing but cry.

Why does it have to hurt so much?

"He doesn't care for you," I yelled at her. Angry tears streamed down my cheeks. "He doesn't give a flying fuck about you. You saw how he kissed her tonight. He fucking doesn't deserve your tears. Just move on already."

Half an hour and another breakdown later, I found my clothes scattered around the floor of my room, a few hanging on the ceiling fan. "I'm stronger than this." These words came out of my mind, while otherwise, I felt like shit. I didn't feel like sleeping. I didn't want to go out either.

I had two months to get over him, but tonight proved I had a long way to go. I just didn't know how to erase the memory of us. Perhaps I'd trusted him too much.

Argh! What's wrong with me? Why can't I just get over him and do my thing?

A distant vibration caught my attention, and I crawled toward my bed, where I had dropped my cell phone earlier. *Mike?*

"Hey." My voice was somewhat bold, but I knew he'd read between the lines without trouble.

"Should you always be this stubborn?" His worried voice filled my ears.

A genuine smile made it to my lips on hearing his voice. That was what friends did, right? Good friends always bring a smile to your lips. "It wasn't a big deal."

"Wasn't it?"

"I'm not going to cry over him, Mike."

"Yeah, and I just rode home on my unicorn."

"Mike..." My voice rang out in warning. I wasn't in a mood to banter. It was already past midnight.

"You need a break. Accept it."

"I need a break."

"Good. I'm coming over tomorrow, and we're leaving for a trip."

Wha--

"But I have to be here for the wedding in three weeks."

"Yeah, whatever."

When he disconnected the call, a deep sigh left my lips, wondering what was on his mind.

Chapter 2

"Ouch!" I cried in shock and rubbed my ass as I blinked to clear my vision.

"Move your sleepy ass before I dunk you in water." Mike's voice infiltrated my still sleepy brain.

"I hate you!"

"Hate me more when I drag you out in this outfit. You have five minutes to change."

"All right. All right." I gave up. There was no point in taking out my fury on him. Knowing Mike, he wouldn't hold back either.

I rubbed my sore ass that still ached from the pinch as I hauled myself to the bathroom, only to pause, noticing everything that had been laid out on the vanity.

"Four minutes." My surprise was answered by another yell from my bedroom.

"A girl needs her time."

"Yes, and we have only an hour left for the flight."

That was enough to rouse my brain. "We're flying where?"

"Three minutes. I don't care if you're naked. You know me."

Shit!

Mike wasn't someone I'd categorize into any stereotypical roles. He was brutally honest and didn't give a damn how others felt about him. Brian once again made his way into my mind as I climbed into the stall for a quick shower. He had even charmed my friends and made them believe he was into me.

"Two minutes!"

My body jerked on hearing Mike's voice, and I welcomed the distraction. Now wasn't the moment to wallow in self-pity. I had no time to apply soap. I quickly dried myself and pulled on the underwear and the floral sundress he'd chosen for me.

"Time's up!"

"I'm coming." I opened the door just in time to see his leg in mid-air. "Must you be always so dramatic?"

Mike shrugged. "That's the only way to handle your stubborn ass."

"I'm not stubborn." I followed him out of the room, and we didn't speak until we reached the threshold.

"Hey, Mike...it's been a long time," Alana's friend Andrea purred. "Are you in a hurry?" she asked when he tried to walk around her.

"Can't you see?" Mike snapped.

"Whoa! There's no need to yell."

"There's every need if you're in my way."

"Well, I was coming to speak to Arianna." She turned her attention to me. "We're going to choose bridesmaid dresses today. Alana wants you to be ready at two p.m." Andrea pivoted on her heel while I was left wondering when I was added to the list.

"She's busy," Mike answered on my behalf. "I'm taking her somewhere."

"Wha—"

We were out the door and in his car before Andrea could finish that sentence. While I didn't like being manhandled, today was different. I appreciated Mike's reaction to her.

"Where are you taking me?"

"Somewhere far."

"How far?"

"Far enough to find the real you."

His response surprised me.

"You've changed a lot in these two months, Ari. You're not you anymore," he said when I didn't respond. "You don't laugh or have fun. Hell, you don't even hang out with us anymore."

"I didn't realize that." My lungs contracted as I processed his words.

"So, this trip is to bring me back?"

"Yes."

"How can you be so sure?"

"You'll see when we get there."

***

The music blared, distracting my thoughts. Mike swatted my hand when I tried to turn the radio off. His eyes challenged me to try again, and my jaw clenched, trying to hold in the retort.

Ever since Brian's betrayal, I stopped listening to music. I didn't know why. I guessed I didn't like the way it made me feel.

"Rule three—never turn off the music when you're in my car."

Yeah, his rules. Men and their cars. Why did they have to love a piece of metal so much? Had they taken care of their women the way they cared for their cars, the relationship could be so much better.

This again brought me to Brian. He loved his Mustang so much that we ended up hailing a taxi instead of driving back from our date. The reason? It rained unexpectedly, and we were drenched. To put it in his words, "The interior will be ruined."

Sometimes, I wondered how I even fell for that guy. He was so different from me. Brian liked jazz, while I loved pop music. While he preferred to waltz, I enjoyed twerking to Nicki Minaj's rap. The differences ran on every level. He loved a three-course dinner, while I was content with a piece of pizza or a burger.

Now I saw why he chose Alana, who shared his likes, but it still didn't explain or justify his betrayal. He could've told me. I had no closure.

"He came of out of his cocoon when he was with you," my subconscious reminded me. True. Brian relaxed after two months of our dating, and he said he could get used to my weirdness. No, he said, "I love your weirdness."

My love-struck brain never processed what he meant at that time. It was now I realized. I was weird to him.

"I'll be forced to lay out new rules during our trip if you keep zoning out."

Mike's annoying voice pulled me out of my depressing thoughts.

"Look, Ari, I don't have experience with breakups. But I will say that he's not worth this suffering."

I looked away, not in a mood to listen.

"You have two choices. Either you can forget him and move on, or you can wallow in self-pity and ruin your life over him." His voice hardened when I choked on a sob. "If you don't stop it, Ari, I swear I'll turn this car around and punch the daylights out of that bastard."

That had my attention. Mike wouldn't hesitate to follow through, and I didn't want that drama. I bit my lip to stop the next sob.

"Good. Now, listen up, sweetheart. I know it won't be easy, but you must do this. You should let this go."

"It isn't easy to erase it all overnight."

"It will never be."

"How do I forget him, Mike?"

Mike shrugged. "Distraction."

Distraction. Yes. But what did he mean by "distraction?"

"Keep yourself busy until you no longer think about him."

Yeah, easier said than done. All I wanted to do was to crawl into a hole and die.

The airport was a twenty-minute drive from my home, and we reached it in less than fifteen minutes thanks to Mike's skillful driving. We walked along the concourse as I fought the memories that sneaked in.

I tried Mike's advice. Distraction. Only it wasn't working how I wanted. Different smells stirred my senses as he herded me toward the gate. The rich scent of coffee beans, cookies, and cakes succeeded in grabbing my attention as we walked past a café.

"We don't have time." Mike dragged me along. "Besides, I've stocked everything you need on the plane."

"Are we flying on your private jet?"

"Isn't that obvious?"

I shrugged, relaxing more. "Where are you taking me, exactly?"

"The Cortez estate."

A pair of cold gray eyes flashed in my memory at the mention of the name. The Cortez estate was located on a private island near New Ikandas, a small yet glorious city that marked the border of the United States and Canada. SeñorCortez's father bought it as a gift to his late wife in the early 1900s. I had been there a handful of times, and it was a wonderful retreat if you were looking for peace.

"Why would you choose the Cortez estate?"

His gaze snapped to mine. "You forgot Enrique's wedding?"

Right. Enrique was finally tying the knot. I vaguely remember Rosie telling me about his wedding, but it had slipped my mind.

"Grandpapa Cortez wants everyone under his roof for Enrique's wedding. You're my third wheel.

A chuckle left my lips. "I can handle that." Mike was engaged to his long-time girlfriend, Skyler. "Is Rosalinda going to be there?"

"Yep."

Our gang wouldn't be complete without her. A real smile stretched my lips when my eyes found the bubbly blonde inside. The recent addition of cherry-red highlights to her hair stood out, and I had to admit it looked cool on her.

"Took you long enough, Ari," she chirped, dragging me to the seat.

"Where's your boyfriend?" I asked.

"On a godforsaken island in the middle of nowhere."

"Oh." That explained her mild irritation. Her boyfriend, Jeff, was an archaeologist.

"You had me worried last night," she complained as I took a seat.

"My phone was—"

"On silent mode. Blah-blah-blah." She rolled her eyes. "Please don't shut us out, Ari. It hurts."

Her voice radiated pain, and I nodded. "I won't."

"So, what's next?"

"No idea. Mike hauled me out of my bed this morning. There was no time to plan."

"That sounds like him. If it helps, he did the same to me. Except he shoved my ass in a taxi."

My eyes felt heavy as I adjusted my position in the seat. A pounding headache from last night returned. Massaging my temples, I reclined in the seat, exhaling as the comfort of sumptuous leather enveloped me. Rosie's hands replaced mine. The mild fragrance of lavender drifted into my nostrils, and a wisp of a smile bloomed on my lips. It felt so good. She continued to rub the diluted oil on my skin.

"What can I do to help?" she whispered, worried.

"You're already helping by being here for me, Rosie." I missed her. Rosie had a job in Seattle, so we didn't see each other as much as we used to. She'd invited me over several times, and I'd been too stubborn.

I focused on her thumb, now circling in a soothing motion on my hand. Having friends like Mike and Rosalinda helped. But how could they help me in my own head?

Before I knew it, my mind was once again shoved into the swirling pit of previously sweet memories that now rose to haunt my days and nights.

"You're very different."

"Good or bad?"

"I don't know." Brian shrugged. "I've never met someone like you before."

"What's your family like?"

"You know them well. My parents have been friends with yours forever."

"Wait, are you telling me you're the Schultz-Schultz?"

"If you put that way, I'm the Schultz-Schultz."

"Your mom hates me!"

"Oh, that's bad."

"What are we gonna do?" I asked, knowing she would never accept someone like me, especially me.

"Doesn't matter." Brian's smile was contagious. "She isn't the one getting married."

"Marriage?" My brows quirked as my heart fluttered.

"Yeah, someday." There was that shy smile on his face again as I pulled his head down. When our lips met, everything felt right.

"Ma'am..."

My eyes shot open as I felt the slight tap on my shoulder, and I blinked to clear my vision. "Hey." My voice was groggy.

"Mr. Frisby ordered this for you." The flight attendant placed a tray before me and left with a professional smile in my direction.

"How long was I out?"

"About two hours."

"Oh."

Uncovering the lid, hot chocolate, chocolate muffins, and sponge cake greeted me. Food certainly was a way to instantly lift your spirits. The delicious aroma coming from that hot chocolate was beckoning me to dive in.

"Skyler is one lucky bitch," Rosie commented as she popped a piece of chocolate muffin in her mouth.

"She is," I agreed. Mike knew how to treat a woman. "So, since we're stuck on the island for the next two weeks, I've made some plans to make the most out of it." Rosie bounced in her seat, pulling out her notepad.

"I'm listening."

"Well, while we're not busy with Enrique's wedding, we can go surfing and skiing."

"Girl, you can't even swim without drowning yourself."

"I heard Orlando hired a sexy lifeguard when he heard we were coming."

The pair of gray eyes flashed again in my mind. Eyes that carried a sadness and anger I could never fathom. Orlando, Mike's maternal cousin and Enrique's elder brother. It felt like ages since I last saw him.

"He's gonna be there." My whisper was barely audible, even to myself. Enrique was more approachable and friendly than Orlando. While Orlando was pleasant to be around, he was always guarded.

I didn't understand why his presence suddenly mattered. It wasn't like we never talked. He was always there at our weekend dinners with

Grandpapa Cortez. The thing was, he was always there. Silent and observing.

"I'm concerned about his yacht and jet skis, not him," Rosie said, distracting me.

"And who's going to convince him?" Orlando rarely allowed anyone to use his jet ski or yacht.

"That's why we have Mike, isn't it? Besides, I'm sure Cortez Senior is easily convinced." She winked.

Grandpapa Cortez was the exact opposite of Orlando. Cheerful, even now. Though he missed his wife dearly, he never let others see or feel his sadness. The old man still visited her grave every day with her favorite flowers. That was how deep their love was.

"Okay. Have it your way, then."

Chapter 3

When we landed at the New Ikandas airport, there was a chopper ready to take us to the estate. I always loved the Cortez family helicopter. Its glass floor gave us the perfect eagle's eye view of the city, an experience one should never miss.

The Cortez family ranked on the list of the top ten billionaires for the past three decades. My dad always wanted to do business with them, but it wasn't easy to get a deal with the Cortezes.

Mike was the only son of Cortez Senior's daughter. Only a few knew of his relationship with the famous family since he had a different surname. Mike, Rosie, and I went to the same school in Linnesse, and we'd been friends since kindergarten.

If my dad knew, he'd have found a way to marry Alana to Mike. I shuddered at the mere thought.

"Say cheese!"

I was pulled out of my reverie by an excited Rosie, and I smiled in time for the selfie. "Are you posting that?"

"Yeah!" Rosie chirped. "The twin pig is stalking me on Instagram. I'm gonna show her that you aren't bawling your eyes out like she expects you to be."

RosalindaPike: On the way to the Cortez Estate with @AriannaSweety320 #Funtime #Relaxed #RetreatToParadise #NewIkandas

Our photo had come out well. New Ikandas did look like a paradise in the background with the vast blue ocean and miniature buildings.

"When did you click that?" I asked, taking the phone from her. It was a photo of me, sleeping, more relaxed in the private jet. There were two more photos, one showing the interior of the plane and the other showing me munching on my muffin.

RosalindaPike: It's time for vacation. Any guesses where we're headed? We're on a private jet, by the way, snacking on chocolate muffins and delicious homemade cookies. #BreakTime #Vacation

There were several comments under the post, and one of them belonged to Alana's friend, Jenna.

Jennalovescookies: Ooh...someone who can't even afford tickets in this economy is now flying in private jet. #JokeOfTheYear

"It's not worth your time, Rosie. They'll always find a way to put you down."

"I know how to handle that bitch. Maybe I should post a reminder of who she is," Rosie said.

*RosalindaPike: You should really stop comparing others with you, Jenna. Maybe if your head isn't stuck up your a** you would've realized earlier that we have actual jobs.*

I rolled my eyes and left her to her gadget, returning back to admiring the scenery before me. It had been a while since I posted anything on my social media. Fortunately, I didn't share the photos of me or Brian anywhere since he wanted no one to find out.

But there was a new photo of them every day on Facebook and Instagram with tons of emojis. I stopped looking at them after a while. It was hurtful to see them, and the photos were a painful reminder of what I lost.

"Look here." Rosie chuckled, showing me the next comment.

Jennalovescookies: Now I know you girls are crazy. No one can go to the Cortez's private estate. Desperate times call for desperate measures.

Honeycake18: Well said, @Jennalovescookies. Nice try, Rosie.

RosalindaPike: That's true @Jennalovescookies, we are indeed desperate to escape from the bitches who were taking up our private space.

Now, this didn't sit well with me. Jenna knew my parents had stopped supporting me since my seventeenth birthday. But I worked in a private firm and had decent savings to afford the trip.

While I didn't like posting my whereabouts on social media, I couldn't help but agree with Rosie. That was two of her friends jumping in, and I wanted to rub it in their faces and show I didn't care.

"Let's go live."

Rosie nodded with a mischievous smile, and I knew right then this would be one hell of a trip.

***

When the chopper landed, we were still laughing. I noticed everyone, including my parents, had joined the live video, though they didn't comment on anything. A secret satisfaction filled me knowing how my parents felt about Cortezes. I pocketed my phone with a satisfied smirk when someone opened the door.

"That smirk is bad news!"

"Enrique!" My grin widened as I jumped into his open arms, squeezing the air out of him. "Congratulations!"

"Thank you. Ah, there's my love. Rosie, sweetheart, give me a hug!"

"You broke my heart, Enrique." I shook my head at her dramatic reply. "You didn't think of me before proposing to Chiara."

My eyes widened when I noticed Jeff, Rosie's boyfriend, creeping up behind her. He placed a finger on his lips, asking me to stay quiet.

"You know I've always loved you," Rosie continued.

"Is that so? Then what about me, my love?"

"Jeff!"

The surprise on Rosie's face was priceless as she jumped into his open arms, kissing him senseless. I recorded the sweet moment on my phone before pocketing it again. I made a note to add this clip to the video I was secretly making to play at her wedding. I knew it was only a matter of time before Jeff proposed. Well, I'd know that since I helped him choose the ring last summer.

"I can't believe you're here." Rosie kept gushing as we walked in.

"I wanted to surprise you, and it worked." Jeff grinned.

"When did you come to Ikandas?"

I tuned out their conversation when I noticed the familiar figure pacing the corridor, phone to his ear. His broad shoulders and tall frame dominated his surroundings, and suddenly, everything around him looked so small.

Dark hair, strong jawline, cold gray eyes, olive-skinned, handsome, and hot as hell—Orlando Gabriele Cortez, the man who never smiled.

When he turned, my breath whooshed out. What was with these men? Age only seemed to increase their hotness. He looked ruggedly handsome with his one-day stubble. His gaze fixated on me as he ended the call and walked toward us.

"Mike! It's great to see you."

"Orlando! It's been a while, cousin."

The men hugged and patted each other's shoulders as I stood there. An awkward feeling filled me as I looked at my crush. It never went very far since Orlando hardly paid me any attention, and I was too young at the time.

"Arianna and Rosalinda, welcome to the Cortez estate." His smile was restricted, and when he held my eyes a moment longer than he usually did, I squirmed under his gaze. He turned to Enrique. "I'm heading to the city. I have to meet the caterers and the wedding planner to make some final arrangements. Tell Papa I'll join him for dinner."

"Sure, brother."

My gaze followed Orlando until he turned and disappeared from view. Now I knew what Mike meant on our way here. Orlando was supposedly my distraction. But did he realize it wouldn't work? I wished their plan didn't add to my "break down and cry" list.

"Orlando doesn't have a plus one to my wedding," Enrique whispered in my ear, making me jump.

"Then let's make sure she's his plus one," Rosie said with a grin.

"What are you guys talking about?" My cheeks had heated up considerably. Orlando could stir my emotions, even after all these years. Maybe that was why the first crush was special. It was a feeling that bloomed in the heart of someone when they were too young to even comprehend what it was. It was also something that made one smile when they looked back at their younger self.

"We know about your crush, girl," Rosie said. "Even after all these years, you get that same look whenever you see him."

I shook my head as Brian's face flashed in my mind. The pain I'd managed to shove away once again made itself known. "And you also know I'm jinxed and never get what I want," I muttered as I walked toward the guest rooms.

Orlando was five years older than I was. He often came to visit Mike and his aunt in Linnesse on the weekends. The estate was their vacation home, and they had a mansion in Linnesse and Ikandas.

While I understood why Orlando wouldn't spare me a second glance, I didn't understand why others would reject me. To Orlando,

I was his cousin's friend. I was younger than he was, and he never saw me the way a man should notice a woman. I was thirteen, and he was eighteen then.

As for the others, they'd always asked me out, only to stand up on me too often to count or ditch me after a few dates. They all wanted the perfect Alana, not me, the flawed, rebellious teen who was shunned by her own family.

"Hey..." Rosie came in as I lay on the bed, aimlessly staring at the ceiling.

"Hey," I greeted without turning to look at her.

"I'm sorry about earlier."

"Don't be."

"You know it isn't true, right?"

"You know it is."

"Ari, I'm sure not all the men are same."

"I believed that when I met Brian." A humorless chuckle bubbled in my throat. "We happened only because he accidentally met me instead of her. Then, when he met her..." I couldn't continue. A sob erupted from the deep pit in my chest and shook my body.

"Oh, baby, he's a fool to let you slip through his fingers."

"He didn't let me slip. He threw me away."

"Ari..."

"What's wrong with me, Rosie? I don't even want to look at my own face anymore. Because all I see is her." We were identical twins, and the more I saw my face, the more I remember. I could only see their betrayal.

Rosie was quiet for a moment. "That's true. You don't look like you anymore."

This had my attention.

"The bastard was changing you without you realizing, Ari. Your hair isn't bouncing like it used to before. You stopped wearing bright colors, and even your dressing style changed over the time you were with him. I was a fool to not notice it earlier."

When her words dawned on me, I rushed to the bathroom, looking at myself. Rosie was right. I couldn't even tell who I was anymore. All this time, I thought I was changing him, but in reality, he was changing me.

I no longer wore my favorite red lipstick. Alana's favorite peach gloss adorned my lips now. I began to straighten my hair so it now looked like hers. The same went for my clothes and accessories.

"Why? Don't you like this dress?"

"I do. I just don't like bright colors," Brian responded, hiding a grimace.

"Oh."

"Hey, I didn't say it doesn't look good. I prefer this instead of your steel bangles," he said, slipping a golden charm bracelet on my hand before removing the steel trinkets I loved.

Brian replaced everything I loved with another thing in the form of a gift, and I never realized it. He was taking control of my life, and I let him, like a fool. Tears flowed freely as I thought about my naivety.

"How about a makeover?" Rosie smirked as she leaned on the frame. At that moment, that sounded like the first thing I needed.

Chapter 4

I sat facing Rosie as she worked on my hair.

"You came prepared," I said, noticing the different shades of hair color packages in her vanity case.

"Yeah. I've been planning a visit ever since your breakup, and when Mike called, I grabbed everything that came to mind." She inspected her bag, producing a catalog of six colors. "So, which one do you want?"

Indecision clouded my mind. The dark shades were appealing. Would it look good? I'd always been a blonde. After contemplating for a moment, I gave up. "Anything that's not her."

"Hmm...something dark, then," she said to herself as she browsed through the packets. "Why don't you close your eyes and relax while I work on you?" she suggested, and I nodded.

A few hours later, I was stunned to see my transformation. My now dark brown hair complimented my honey-brown eyes, and it was now cut into layers. Though nothing would change much, it brought a sense of relief.

The day had surprisingly been relaxing, and I felt a lot better after my makeover. Being able to see myself in the mirror without remembering her face was a relief. A sigh left my lips as a liberated feeling lifted my spirits. I couldn't take my eyes off the mirror as I traced my face with the first real smile in a long time.

Our lunch and evening snacks were delivered to our room. When I opened the bags Mike packed for me, I was surprised to notice he had packed the clothes I preferred to wear before meeting Brian.

I chose my dark purple floor-length dress. Dinner at the Cortez estate was a family event. Grandpapa Cortez expected everyone at the table. Just as I was about to strip, the door burst open, and Skyler entered with a bubbly Chiara.

"Wow!" Skyler's eyes went wide as she noticed my appearance. "You are absolutely gorgeous. Not that you weren't before, but I love this look."

"Thanks."

"I'm sorry I wasn't here when you guys arrived. Thanks for coming on such short notice." Chiara sat on the bed, letting out a loud exhale.

"Notice?" Rosie snorted. "Girl, we didn't even know we were coming here until Mike hauled our asses onto his jet."

"That sounds like him." Skyler chuckled.

"We're happy to be here, though." Rosie shrugged and continued to highlight her cheekbones. The talk turned to the upcoming wedding while I changed.

"All right, we have to get ready for dinner." Chiara and Skyler excused themselves after a while, leaving us alone.

Rosie offered to curl my hair. Thoughts of Brian slipped in and out, but I was managing better than I expected.

"There you go," she said when she finished curling the last strands.

When we arrived at the dinner table, I was flustered to find my seat next to Orlando.

"Ari, here," Mike hollered, patting the seat with a wink. Skyler sat on his right, and the seat on his left, which was on the right-hand side of Orlando, was empty. Enrique and Rosalinda sat on the opposite side.

"Arianna, you look lovely, my dear," Cortez Senior greeted from the head of the table. His son, Ricardo, Orlando and Enrique's father, gave me a tight-lipped smile.

"Thank you, Grandpapa. You aren't bad yourself. I see where the Cortez handsomeness comes from."

"So, you agree we are handsome," Enrique said smugly.

"Never claimed you weren't. Except I wish you had inherited a brain similar to Grandpapa too," I retorted, once again feeling like my old self.

The table boomed with laughter, and my cheeks heated when I noticed Orlando looking at me in my peripheral vision. The amused look on his face was something I had never seen before.

"You sure know how to boost an old man's ego, Arianna." Señor Cortez chuckled. "I like your new look. It suits your personality, bold and elegant."

"I agree. The dark color suits her well," Orlando commented, making my heart stutter.

"Thank you." I smiled and focused on the food on my plate.

"Chiara, when is your family coming?" Uncle Rick asked.

"Next week, Papa."

"Orlando, have you made necessary arrangements for their stay?"

"Yes, Papa."

"Good."

Grandpapa Cortez cleared his throat. "Tonight, I'd like to toast." He picked up his glass. "To Enrique and his lovely bride-to-be, Chiara."

Everyone raised their glasses of champagne while I raised my water. On my left, Orlando did the same, and we laughed, a short, amused chuckle from me and a deep rumble I barely heard from him. A second later, his cold mask was on again, making me wonder if I imagined it.

"Arianna," Chiara called.

"Yes."

"There's something I wanted to ask you and Rosalinda. Will you both be my bridesmaids?"

"And you ask this after arranging everything, including my dress for the wedding?"

Chiara grinned sheepishly and raised her arms in surrender. "I was sure you wouldn't say no. Don't make me beg, please…"

"You don't have to Chiara. You're one of us now." Rosie waved her hand. "Besides, we wouldn't miss it for anything."

"That's great." Enrique clapped. "Arianna can be Orlando's plus one for the wedding."

The others at the table stiffened for a moment, and I noticed Orlando's hand clenching around his glass. He glared at Enrique. If looks could kill, Enrique would be dead now.

"It won't be necessary," I piped in, trying to hide my nervousness. "I'll go alone."

"You don't have a choice," Mike snapped. "If Orlando doesn't want to go with you, then you can be my third wheel. I'm sure Skyler wouldn't mind."

I hit his arm with a playful grin and masked the hurt. *You'll never be someone's special one, Arianna.* My twin's words surfaced, making my smile falter. She was right. I'd always be a third wheel.

Orlando didn't speak as we continued to eat. I could feel his occasional glances at me. Everyone chatted normally while I withdrew to my own world. This made me think about all the times we had dinner at this table before. Orlando was the only one who'd stay quiet while we bickered back and forth. It made me wonder if Orlando had a broken past.

He wasn't always like this. Orlando used to banter, laugh, and play. We had fun during our first trip here, during a summer vacation after my seventh-grade year. Orlando spent his break with us before leaving for college.

The second time I saw him was after I finished high school. We came to the estate to spend our break, and Orlando was here, barely talking. He'd been closed off ever since.

I had seen him several times after starting college when he came to Mike's home on weekends. But he'd turned silent. The eyes, which once glinted with mischief, now only held a cold anger.

Is it a woman?

I'd probably never know. Mike would've said something if he knew. But again, it felt as if a puzzle piece clicked in place. I'd never tried to think about it this way. The men tried to talk to Orlando about it, but he had shut them out. Deep in my heart, I just knew he was hurt. When I couldn't stomach the food anymore, I stood, excusing myself from the table and faking a yawn.

"Why can't you be her plus one?" I heard Enrique snap.

"She can invite Brian," Orlando hissed as I exited the door and took a right. "You didn't have to push this in my face."

"They're not together anymore, dammit!" Mike's voice boomed. "I thought you knew that already."

I increased my pace, not wanting to hear anything being said. Somehow, I knew this was coming. Orlando hadn't been seen with a woman in years. Mike never said he had a girlfriend.

Instead of distracting me, this trip only increased my stress. I could only guess how much trouble it would put me through in the next two weeks; *so much for my getaway plan.*

Suddenly, it felt like I was stuck with no escape. All the things I tried so hard to forget were coming at me in full force. I understood they were trying to help. But it didn't work that way, did it? Orlando couldn't be the cure to my pain.

"Arianna!"

I whipped around, almost losing my balance as my heel caught on the hem of my long dress, tripping me in the process. Orlando closed the distance between us when I barely saved myself from another embarrassment.

"Hey," I mumbled.

"You okay?"

"Yeah, I'm fine..." I composed myself and cleared my throat.

"I'm sorry about earlier. I wasn't expecting that, and I didn't know about..." His eyes locked with mine as he contemplated his next words.

"It's fine."

His features softened. "So, will you be my date for Enrique's wedding?"

"You don't have to do this."

"I was upset because I wasn't informed about this earlier, and I had no chance to ask you properly. You deserve nothing less."

My breath hitched, and I blinked, unable to believe what he was saying. "It's okay. Really."

"It's not okay, Arianna. It's not that I don't want to go with you. If we are going together, then I'm doing it the right way. I'll ask you again." His posture relaxed, and he thrust his hands inside his pant pockets. "Will you be my date to the wedding?"

"Um..." My heart raced. "Ah...yes, sure." I smiled nervously. He didn't have to do this, and I was touched by his kind gesture. My mind raced, bringing up unpleasant memories without warning.

Hot tears burned my eyes when I remember how Brian would avoid taking me to public events. Shortly before he proposed to Alana, he began taking her to the parties as his plus one. When I confronted him, he said it was his mother's request and they were merely representing their business and nothing more.

"Good." Orlando smiled. "Come, I'll walk you to the door."

"That's...um...you don't have to do that." I shifted from one foot to the other and averted my face to hide my tears. If Orlando noticed, his expression didn't show it.

"I told you earlier, Arianna. You're my date, and I want to do it the right way. Let me do this, please."

The words of protest died in my throat, and I pivoted on my heel. Orlando followed closely. His cologne drowned me, and his presence made me self-conscious. When we reached the door, I stopped, unsure what to do next.

"Good night, Arianna."

Orlando stood there, hands still in his pockets, as he looked down at me.

A small drop of disappointment filled me when I realized he was just being nice. I had to smack my confused brain for getting distracted like this. *You're here to forget Brian,* I told myself.

"Good night," I whispered, meeting his eyes for one last time before entering the room.

Chapter 5

As soon as I stepped into the loneliness of my room, the composure I'd managed to pull together crumbled. I relieved a pained breath as I made my way to the bed.

My fingers massaged my temples as I lay there with no will to change. I couldn't comprehend why I reacted to Orlando like this. After all, we were never an item. He'd been my childhood crush, nothing more. I was sure every teen girl had one. The crush I had on Orlando was like the crush one would have over their favorite movie star.

Yes, that's it.

You're overreacting, Arianna.

My hands found the phone that was carelessly tossed on the bed. Several notifications on my Instagram beckoned me. Opening the app, I noticed several comments about our trip, mostly about how beautiful the place was and how lucky we were.

There were more photos from Alana and Brian, snippets from their pre-wedding photoshoot. I was tempted to unfollow and block them, but I didn't. I should stop looking, but I also had to remind myself why I shouldn't break down.

That was what they would expect, for me to break down. I wouldn't give them that satisfaction.

"I'm stronger than this. I was happier before I met Brian. I can be happy again." Chanting this mantra, I made my way to the closet to change for bed.

The warm bed and comfortable sheets were no comfort to my racing mind. No matter how much I tried, I couldn't rein in my thoughts. They were now occupied by Brian and Alana.

I didn't know what I did wrong for my parents to hate me so much. Hatred was an understatement. After my wild party on my seventeenth birthday, they gradually stopped talking altogether.

Mom once confronted me, but she was never one to listen. She heard half and assumed the rest. The conversation didn't end well because she kept blaming me despite my apologies. And I politely asked her to fuck off. She stormed off that day and never talked to me again. Dad––he rarely talks and always listens to Mom.

I shouldn't have hosted the party, I agreed. And I shouldn't have drunk before I was legal. But it wasn't a big deal like they said. I never realized paparazzi had slipped into our private party and taken photos.

That night, I was wasted before I knew it, and Mike had locked me in a room with Rosalinda. Mike, who was sober, made sure our innocence wasn't ruined in a drunken haste.

We woke up with massive hangovers and stinky clothes amidst our own vomit. The stink and the cleaning process aftermath taught me a lesson I would never forget. Mike showed us a few photos of our unconscious state, and I vowed never to lose control again. I never touched alcohol in my life after that night. I'd rather deal with all the shit in my life than dealing with hundreds of hammers pelting my head all day long. Also, the concept of losing control didn't sit well with me. I, for one, liked the control I had over my life.

I wondered why I thought about that incident all of a sudden. My thoughts wandered back to Brian and how surprised he was when he learned I didn't drink.

"What's there to be surprised about?"

"Nothing." Brian smiled. *"I just can't believe you don't drink."*

"Oh, right. Why does everyone always assume things that way?"

"Maybe it's because of your rebellious nature?" His statement was more like a question.

Does he think I am rebellious? *"I'm not rebellious, Brian. I'm a girl who likes to live her life without being told what to do and how to do it. I hate when someone constantly breathes down my neck with advice. I'm twenty-four, and I firmly believe I know how to differentiate right and wrong."*

"I get it." Brian lifted his hands in surrender. "That's something I love about you." His smile was genuine. "You're always yourself, and I like that." There was a longing in his voice. "With you, I feel like I can be myself and don't have to think twice about what others think of me."

"You're perfect the way you are, Brian. You shouldn't change for anyone else."

"Thank you."

I jerked out of my thoughts and wiped off the tears that had accumulated. The bedroom walls were suffocating me all of a sudden, and I had to get out. My body moved of its own accord to get out of the bed. I grabbed the huge, fluffy blanket to keep me warm and slipped on my flats as I exited the room.

The cold air of New Ikandas hit me as soon as I stepped out of the warmth of the mansion. Goose bumps erupted on my skin, where it was kissed by the air. A shiver ran through my body as I continued to walk to the beach.

The path to the beach was lit by lampposts on both sides. LED lights illuminated the greens and made it look like a paradise at night. I could see the lighthouse not so far away as the sound of the ocean waves wrapped my mind with calm.

This was something I liked about this estate. It was never dark. The Cortezes had good taste in designing the interiors and landscape. Even now, the entire place looked like a mystical garden. Every aspect about it was so calming.

The fragrance of a white flower I didn't know the name of greeted me as soon as I rounded the corner. Mike said they had imported the plants from India, and they had a mesmerizing scent that calmed me. It was a pleasant mixture of the cool air and the sound of waves––a perfect treat to all my senses.

My hold on the blanket tightened as I made my way to the beach. The sand tempted me to ditch my flats, but the seeping cold kept my temptation in check. I wasn't a fan of cold, but now it was needed to numb my nerves.

At the dinner table, I was tempted to touch alcohol again. But I made a promise that I wouldn't ruin myself over Brian. I was happy before him. It was only a matter of finding out how to be happy again. I wondered if I'd be so miserable if he had broken up with me prior to all this.

A deep sigh left my lips, and the air puffed out as if I were smoking, something my childish self had enjoyed. The thing about Ikandas, the climate was moderate throughout the year. The summers weren't too hot, and the winters weren't too cold.

In the distance, city lights glittered in the night. The estate was located on an island a few miles offshore, with the city on one side and the open sea on the other, with a vast beach. It was the perfect location for a wedding.

The Cortez family also rented the beach for destination weddings occasionally. The only way to get to the island was through the air or through the water. It covered roughly a hundred acres of land and vegetation. There were no wild animals, which was a relief. However, Mike had told me that their estate was an ideal location for migrating birds. The estate would be open for bird lovers and tourists during the day.

"Beautiful, isn't it?"

A scream tore through the night, and I realized it was mine when a large hand covered my mouth. I jumped as my grip on the blanket slipped, and my body came in contact with a much colder one.

"Shh, it's me," Orlando said when I struggled in his hold.

My body stopped thrashing immediately as hot air fanned my neck. His hold relaxed, and my heart fluttered again. *Did he follow me?*

"What are you doing here?" he asked as I stepped away and picked the blanket from the ground.

"I couldn't sleep." The distant light illuminated his perfectly sculpted face, and I swallowed, realizing I was staring at him. He was shirtless, with only a pair of shorts covering him. The way they hung low on his hips didn't help either.

Orlando nodded in understanding and turned to walk away. After contemplating for a moment, I decided to follow him. Suddenly, his presence felt good.

"You're cold," I said as he took a seat on one of the benches laid out on the beach.

"I'm used to it."

"My blanket is huge enough for both of us," I suggested as I took a seat beside him. I didn't wait before I threw one end of the blanket over his shoulder and brought it around us to hold it together. I shivered from the cold radiating from his body. "You're freezing."

A contented sigh left his lips, and they stretched, forming a smile. My heart lurched, seeing how young and handsome it made him look. We sat there in silence, admiring the waves for a while before he spoke again.

"So, Mike said you resigned your job. What happened?"

"Brian happened." I didn't hesitate. They all knew about him. In fact, it was my dream to get married on this estate––an excellent wedding and honeymoon.

"You broke up with him?"

"No. He dumped me for my sister. They're getting married in three weeks." My voice held the pain that was still raw inside my chest.

"Asshole."

I chuckled. "And he didn't even bother to break up with me."

"When did you find out?"

"Two months ago, when he showed up for one of our family parties," I drawled. "He proposed to her in front of everyone."

I still remember that day. Brian had said his family was sending him on a business trip, and he was going to visit their overseas branches. It was the first time he was going away, and I remember how miserable I was when I gave him a teary send-off. Now, when I thought about it, it was the same time my parents sent Alana abroad for the first time. "You are our heir. It's time you got involved in the family business," I'd heard Mom say to her.

At that time, nothing crossed my mind. When they both returned two months later, I first experienced the taste of betrayal. The party was hosted in her honor. Dad announced her as his successor, and then Brian showed up. My foolish heart fluttered at the sight, and I wanted to run into his arms and smother him with kisses.

But then he didn't even glance in my direction. He went to my parents, and greeted them. They spoke in hushed voices before Brian clinked his glass to grab everyone's attention. When he began speaking, my heart was a nervous mush.

"You know, that night at the party when he began telling everyone how he met the girl of his dreams and how much he loved her, I thought he was talking about me. I believed he finally got his parents' blessing and was going to surprise me."

I could still recall that elevated feeling that made it seem like my body was floating on hearing his words. Sobs threatened to spill as I realized what was happening. I never realized the happiness would be sucked away and I'd be pushed into a void of no return.

"Then he got on one knee and said her name." My voice broke and my body heaved with a violent sob. "He said, 'Alana, my love, will you make me a proud man by becoming my wife?'" I recalled his exact words.

Orlando's hands enclosed me and rubbed my back as I continued to sob.

The crowd erupted into claps and cheers when those words left Brian's mouth. It felt as if I had plunged face-first from a building. Did I hear that right? *I blinked several times and tried to comprehend what I just heard.* Alana, not Arianna.

Alana giggled and made her way toward him in slow motion as I stood frozen. "Yes!" she screamed as our parents squealed with joy. My stupid, love-struck brain couldn't understand what my vision was transferring to it. My twin was now kissing my boyfriend.

"I don't remember how I made it to my room. I was numb." Brian stayed over that night, which I found out in the morning, and for several nights after their high-profile engagement. It was the next night I confronted him.

Chapter 6

The cold breeze kissed my face as I gazed off into the distance, listening to the sounds of the sea.

Orlando continued to rub my back, his fingers circling soothingly. "A month ago, there was a request to the estate office for a beach wedding. I didn't accept it since Enrique's wedding is planned here, and he wanted the beach guesthouse for his honeymoon."

This information had me perked up. *Brian, that bastard.* "Is it them?"

"Brian Schultz and Alana Swanson." He nodded. "Your father called me personally when I declined their initial request."

Tears accumulated again as this news hit home. Brian knew this estate was my retreat. "I wanted to get married here." My voice was barely a whisper.

Orlando shifted, facing me as his hands circled my body. I wiped my tears and looked away when his thumb started rubbing my right hand.

"There's a vacancy in one of my companies if you're interested," he said. "You can stay at the staff quarters if you want to."

I appreciated the change of subject and nodded. "I'd love that." I knew about all their businesses and didn't have to think twice. In fact, I was planning to ask Mike myself. Orlando was so close, his strong shoulders inches away. Without thinking, I leaned my head on his shoulder, taking in all the comfort he was offering.

"What's your story?" I asked him after a few moments of silence.

His body stiffened, confirming my suspicions. "I don't have a story." His voice was clipped, distant.

"I want to forget," I said, dropping the subject that seemed to upset his mood. "I refuse to cry, and I don't want to ruin my life over him. This trip is supposed to be a distraction, but when I'm alone, all I can think is about him."

I wasn't expecting a response. He wasn't much of a talker, but he listened well. Orlando had always kept to himself. I never understood why.

But this time was different. It seemed like I could feel his pain. I understood the emotion behind his permanent cold glare and knew he was hurt once. He seemed to understand me, and maybe that was what brought him closer. I was sure the others were noticing the changes in him. Orlando has always been around me since my arrival.

"What did you do?" I pressed, treading carefully. I thought maybe opening myself to him would make him talk.

"I worked." His voice was a whisper. "I drowned myself in work until I could no longer keep my eyes open."

I wondered if he'd ever talked about it before. Silence once again stretched between us. Comfortable.

Orlando rested his chin on top of my head, and I realized I was leaning on his chest. *So warm.* Somewhere during the conversation, I must've shifted. He adjusted my body in his arms, an intimate action done as if this were a normal occurrence between us.

I didn't dwell much on this closeness. My eyes fluttered as the cold air and his warmth lulled me. His thumb still traced circles on my hand. The pain in my heart lessened as the circles continued. Before I knew it, I drifted off to sleep.

***

My heart and head felt light when I stretched under the cozy blankets. The softness of the bed had me swooning. I snuggled deeper, inhaling the mild citrus scent on the sheet that relaxed me further. It was like any other day before Brian.

That name. I sat up as if a bucket of cold water had splashed on me. How did I get here? I reminisced my walk to the beach and falling asleep in Orlando's arms.

I couldn't believe in one night we had gone from being complete strangers to something more. There was an unspoken understanding between us last night. He listened to me, and his touch was like a balm to my aching heart. There was nothing sexual about that touch. Just comfort. Orlando must've brought me here.

My phone rang, causing me to shake my thoughts and search for it. Finding it under the bed, I cursed, seeing who it was. "Hey..."

"Arianna, oh, sweetie. You had us all worried. What were you thinking?" The chastising voice belonged to Mike's mother, Gabriella.

"I'm sorry." I felt like crap for shutting her out.

"Mike told me what happened." Her voice cracked on the other end as I suppressed my tears. Suddenly, I wanted to sink myself in her embrace and let go. Hearing her voice reminded me how much I missed her. "When I found out, I wanted to come down and wring his neck. How dare he mess with my daughter like that?" My tears flowed freely now. "Mike wouldn't let me. He said you wouldn't want all that drama."

No, I wouldn't.

"But I swear, Ari, when I see that bastard again, he'll remember why he shouldn't cross my daughters ever again."

Gabriella always referred to me and Rosie as her daughters. Her love was fierce, and Mike was every bit like her. So, I knew she wouldn't hesitate to follow through on her words.

Her voice softened. "Tell me you're okay, sweetie."

"I'm okay," I sniffled.

"I was so furious that I called Orlando to arrange my itinerary when you didn't answer. Then he said you were fine, and he'll make sure you talked with me before I came over."

There she went again. Her words brought a smile to my lips. The woman talked a lot, and I loved her to bits.

"You're smothering her, Gaby." Uncle Frisby's voice rang in the background, the only voice of reason in the Frisby household. "Shouldn't you let her say something?"

"You better shut it, Frisby, else you'll be in the doghouse for the next two weeks."

I coughed, trying to hide my discomfort.

"If you cared, you would've persuaded her to move in with us. Mike hauled her ass out of that wretched place."

I could imagine him rolling his eyes as he immersed himself in the newspaper or a book. No one talked when the mom or son threw tantrums, and rightly so. Her attention switched. "Ari, why wouldn't you come? Mike said you refused to leave when he called."

Why? My throat constricted. "I didn't want to be a coward." Alana and her friends would laugh and take pleasure in my leaving. I didn't want her to think I couldn't handle a breakup.

"Aww...sweetie. Did I ever tell you how much you remind me of my younger self?"

Yes, she said it almost every time we met.

"Don't you ever put yourself in a situation like this ever again. Do you understand? If something happened, you come straight to us."

I knew that. Mike and his family would always have my back. "I love you, Gaby."

Gabriella exhaled. "I love you too, Ari. Please take of yourself and that grumpy godson of mine, will you?"

Huh? I almost choked on my saliva and stared at the phone in disbelief. How did she know? Mike. I heard her snicker when the call ended.

Ugh! What's with everyone?

"The princess is up!"

I whipped around to see Rosie entering the room with a mischievous smile and frowned.

"What's with the smile?"

"Enough with the innocent act, Ari. We saw, all right." She rolled her eyes and plopped beside me on the bed.

"What did you see?"

"Well, we saw how you snuck to the beach at midnight and how Orlando returned with you in his arms an hour later."

My eyes grew wider. I didn't see them anywhere.

"After dinner, we went to the rooftop for some drinks and ended up chatting for a little longer. We saw you going out." She paused, gauging my reaction. "I was about to come after you when Enrique stopped me. He said Orlando would already be there. So, we figured you were meeting him." Her eyebrows wiggled as she nudged me in the ribs. "That was fast."

I shook my head and couldn't help the smile that stretched my lips. "Sorry to burst your bubble. Nothing is happening between us."

"But..."

"I didn't know he'd be there. It was a coincidence, and we ended up talking. Well, I talked, and he listened. Then I fell asleep." I intentionally avoided the cuddling part since I didn't want her to get any ideas. It was too soon, and I wasn't even over Brian yet.

"That's okay. At least you guys talked. I'm sure things are going to work out differently for you."

"Please don't go there, Rosie."

"It's not easy, but not impossible either. You remember how pathetic and messy I was when I broke up with Gage?"

I did. That idiot cheated on her and laughed in her face when she confronted him. It happened during our first year of college. Rosie was heartbroken. She'd thought she'd found the one, just like I thought Brian was the one for me.

Rosie combed my untamed hair with her fingers as a sigh of contentment escaped my lips.

"I'm scared, Rosie."

"It's okay to be scared, sweetie. Do what you have to do. But remember, you won't let them have the last laugh."

I nodded and snuggled against her as the first round of tears for that day soaked her shirt.

***

When I made it to the dining room for lunch, everyone had already started. Once again, the chair beside Orlando was empty. Mike grinned, patting that seat, and I suppressed the urge to shake my head at his pettiness.

Orlando sported a small smile when our eyes met, and I nodded, acknowledging his silent greeting.

"The wedding is barely a week away. Is everything set, Orlando?" Ricardo asked, his gray eyes boring into his son.

"Everything is arranged, Papa. I've also rented two luxury yachts to transport guests for the wedding."

Ricardo turned to Enrique. "Is everything to your liking, son?" His voice and features softened when he spoke to his younger son.

"It is, Papa. Orlando and the wedding planner have done a great job. I can't imagine anything more perfect than this." Enrique squeezed Chiara's hand.

"Good." Ricardo smiled a little, and I realized how similar Orlando's smile was to his father's.

"Where do the guests stay after the wedding?" Grandpapa Cortez asked.

"We've reserved rooms in one of our hotels in the city, Grandpapa," Orlando answered. "I've also hired an agency to supervise the security, so it'll strictly be a family affair."

Grandpapa and Ricardo nodded while I could feel an invisible tension mounting. And I couldn't help but notice how Orlando's jaw clenched when he mentioned it would strictly be a family affair.

***

"Mike, what's with all this tension?" I asked on our way to the beach. Everyone else was walking ahead of us. Skyler and Chiara had their arms around Rosie's neck as they argued about something.

"You noticed that, huh?" Mike stared at the sea that now glittered like blue diamonds kissed by the afternoon sun. The warm air was pleasant. "How much do you want to know?"

"As much as I need to understand what this is all about."

"Well, Uncle Rick's wife ran off with her secret lover when Enrique was only three months old."

"Oh." That explained why they never spoke about her.

"Uncle Ricardo was a wreck. Their divorce was very ugly and very public. She claimed he was abusing her. He was arrested but released since there was no evidence. When she found she wouldn't get a dime from him, she went on to claim the children weren't his. It became a mess when she drew the media in. Orlando and Enrique mostly grew up with me in our household until the press got tired of hounding them."

Wow. I could only imagine what Orlando went through as a child. At least Mike's mother, Gabriella, was there for the siblings. She was a kindhearted soul. She was also the only maternal figure in my life. "Do you think she'll cause trouble at the wedding?"

"She'll never cease to use an opportunity. The Cortez family, including us, have a restraining order against her."

"Why is she here now?"

"It's complicated and not something I'm sure Orlando would want me to share. I can say he's doing his best to keep this under wraps. The press wouldn't let go of this if they found out."

That woman was a character. It explained why Ricardo remained single.

"Does Orlando have a girlfriend?"

Mike paused, and his brows creased as he gave me a once-over. His posture relaxed as a playful smirk found its way to his mouth. "Girlfriend, eh?" He shrugged. "He's single. As for his past relationships, he's pretty secretive about it."

It wasn't something I was expecting, but it would do. Why would I care, anyway? It wasn't like we were dating. I was here to distract myself from the pain and heartbreak of my sister marrying my ex. I needed to stick to the original plan.

Sticking my nose in Orlando's business promised heartbreak. I was content with his friendship and the understanding we had. I didn't want to lose it. I didn't know why, but just the thought of him not talking to me caused an ache in my heart.

"Ari..." Mike called in a hesitant voice. "Look, you know I'd be more than happy if you and Orlando ended up together. But just don't get too comfortable with this thing you're starting, okay?"

"I don't understand." In contrast to my words, my mind understood exactly what he was talking about. He didn't want me to fall for Orlando. The logical side of my brain said one couldn't fall for someone immediately after a breakup. I wasn't really concerned at this point. How could I fall for Orlando when I still couldn't get over Brian?

"Look, he might not be even around once this wedding is over. Ari, it's natural for an aching soul to reach out. But Orlando, I don't think he's ready for that step."

"So, you do know about his past."

"Not really. We..." He scratched his chin and looked around, making sure no one was nearby. His voice lowered. "We have a theory. Orlando was happier than ever when he came home for spring break. Then, the next time he came, he was a changed man. We know a girl is involved. Whatever happened, he never got over it."

"Okay." It was easier to connect the dots now. Orlando's breakup must've been worse than mine. What happened? Did she cheat on him?

"Listen, if this thing between you works out, I'll be the happiest person alive. But I'm not sure how to feel about this. You're my best friend, and he's my cousin. If something went wrong––" He took a deep breath, shaking his head. "Just be careful, okay?"

I nodded. My thoughts galloped, imagining different scenarios. *Ugh! Shut it, Arianna. Focus on the present.*

"All right, come here." Mike pulled me into his embrace.

I sighed contentedly as his strength surrounded me. His hand encased my head just like my dad used to do when I was little. I never knew why it stopped. Maybe that was why God sent me Mike. "I love you. I don't know what I would've done without you or Rosie," I said, burying my face against his chest. I grabbed his t-shirt, bunching it in my fist.

"I love you too, and we'll always be here for you," Mike whispered and kissed the crown of my head. "Now go and have some fun."

Chapter 7

"Distraction tip of the day: live in the present and enjoy the moment. Worry about the depressing stuff later." Rosie's cheerful voice pulled me out of my thoughts as I made my way to the beach.

I smiled and took a deep breath, realizing the others were closer. "How long did it take for you to move on?"

"I don't remember." Rosie shrugged. "I guess the pain is always there. But now that I have Jeff, I always think of how blessed I am to have him whenever I remember Gage."

I nodded. It sounded like a logical answer.

"Just live one day at a time, Ari. When you remember the pain, distract yourself with something that helps you to forget it enough to get through the day."

Her words made sense, and I felt like it was doable. I could certainly do that. *Distract myself with something...*

My eyes found the epitome of male hotness walking toward our little group. The afternoon sunlight kissed his glistening olive skin.

"That'll work too," Rosie smirked. "He's hot."

"Rosie!" I pinched her arm.

"Ouch!" she hissed. "What? I was just saying."

I shook my head and turned away, averting my gaze from the distracting presence behind me. I was distracted, all right. But the small butterflies that fluttered in my lower belly every time I saw him were what scared me the most.

My insides fluttered when I met Brian too. But this was intense. Orlando's mere presence affected me like no other. It dominated me and made me want to do things I'd only dreamed of doing.

"Hundred bucks––you'll kiss your V-card goodbye before we leave this island."

I whipped around, meeting Rosie's playful yet confident grin. For the first time, there were no words of protest in my mouth. I became embarrassed as what she implied finally dawned on me.

"You didn't object." Her grin grew wider.

It was true. Every time she made that prediction about me and Brian, I always objected, saying I wasn't ready and wanted to wait. Now that I thought about it, I was glad I waited.

"Enrique said you guys wanted to ride the jet ski." Orlando's voice made goosebumps erupt on my skin.

"Yeah!" the girls all chorused.

"There are four, and my yacht is docked at Northwest. I've arranged dinner and a cocktail party for you guys in honor of the bride and groom," Orlando announced.

"Cool!" Jeff said.

"Since you all decided to hang out at the beach, I've arranged refreshments. The jet skis are there if you want to ride one now. Don't forget to wear a life jacket, and guards are stationed around the area if you need help."

"We'll swim and hang out for now," Mike said. "What about you guys?"

The girls debated, weighing their choices, and decided on swimming first. "We're in," Rosie announced.

"Who's going to join me?" Enrique called as he ran toward the water.

"Live in the moment, girl." Rosie nudged me before racing after the others toward the sea, leaving me with Orlando.

"Aren't you going with them?"

"Um...no."

"Your skin is pink," he observed, mistaking my discomfort for the sun's heat. His hand traced my arm. "Come. There's sunscreen here." He led me to one of the beach chairs and handed me the sunscreen lotion from the small table beside it. The umbrella provided us with a perfect shade.

"Thanks." I poured a generous amount into my hand before applying it over my arms and face. It wasn't too hot, but the humidity was making me sweaty. I turned around and took off my loose sleeveless top, revealing my peach-colored bikini top.

I pulled out my phone from my trousers and placed it on the table beside the refreshments. When I began applying the lotion on my front, I felt a strong hand on my shoulders. It wasn't calloused, but the texture was something I'd gotten acquainted with very recently.

My heart skipped a beat as Orlando took the bottle from my hand and squirted some into his large palms. I suppressed a gasp and tried to act normal when he applied the lotion on my back.

"So, what did Rosie say before she took off?" His question pulled me out of the haze his touch was lulling me into.

"To live at the moment," I blurted.

Orlando hummed and quickly finished applying the lotion, and I clamped my lips shut to keep the protest from escaping when his hands left my body.

"I thought you didn't allow others to use your jet ski," I said, remembering Rosie mentioning it earlier.

"That was because Enrique had an accident two years ago. He was drunk at the time, and we almost lost him."

"Oh. Where's the yacht? I don't see one."

"It's on the other side," he said. The part of the beach where we were was actually like a private cove. It was partially hidden, and the curved shoreline gave us privacy. There was a pier on the other side along the beach that was occasionally rented to the guests.

"Do you want to swim?"

"No. I'll just hang out here."

"Okay." He got up and walked away without another word.

My expression fell because I hoped he'd stay for a chat. A sudden thought crossed my mind as I watched Orlando stretch at the edge of the water. The waves brushed his feet. The wind tousled his hair, and his swim trunks hung low on his hips.

I grabbed my phone and clicked his photo, the high-resolution camera capturing all his hotness into one small frame, the contours of his taut muscles now more prominent.

@AriannaSweety320: A view of Oasis #RetreatToParadise #NewIkandas with @RosalindaPike.

I smirked as I clicked the share button on my Instagram. *It's just to show them I'm not hung up on Brian,* I told myself as I placed the phone on the table again. *Is it?* Okay, maybe I wanted them to burn with envy.

I shook my head and focused on the couples playing in the shallow water. Their laughter reached my ears, and a smile tugged at my lips. I tried not to remember the time I spent with Brian at the beach, but I failed, and my mind was once again sucked to that day.

"Hey, aren't you gonna swim?"

"No. I'll just hang out for a while." His expression turned sour when he noticed my bikini.

The two-piece swimming garment was modest to me, but he didn't agree. Instead of admiring me like I thought he would, he threw his t-shirt at me and asked me to wear it.

"We are on a beach, Brian."

"That piece barely covers your body, Arianna. What were you thinking?"

"I can't swim with all my clothes on."

Brian pinched the bridge of his nose and clenched his jaw. "Listen, honey, our family has a reputation to uphold. My parents would have a heart attack if they see you like this. What if the paparazzi shows up? You shouldn't wear this in public."

"You can't tell me how I should dress, Brian. I'm capable of making my own choices, and I'm dating you, not your parents."

That was the incident that led to our first fight. I had changed so much for him and gave preferences to his choices, but he kept dictating everything I did. It was becoming too much, but like the fool I was, I tried to fit in.

A sudden splash of water brought me out of my thoughts, soaking my upper body, and before I knew it, I was being hoisted from my seat.

"Mike!" I gasped, wiping the water off my face.

"I warned you not to zone out. For that, you'll be punished."

My eyes widened when I realized what he was about to do. "Mike, no, I don't want my hair wet."

"Too late!"

My surprised squeak was answered with sounds of laughter and splashing, followed by saltwater stinging my eyes and entering my nostrils. I shot out of the water, gagging.

"I hate you."

"You're welcome!" Mike was already swimming away, leaving me with the girls.

"So…" Chiara grinned and wiggled her eyebrows.

"That wasn't a pleasant experience," I snapped.

"She meant the exchange between you and our grumpy-pants, there." Skyler pointed at Orlando, who I noticed was now drinking a beer with the guys.

"Can't they drink that on the shore?" I frowned.

Skyler quirked her eyebrows, not pleased with me evading her question. I looked at Rosie for support, and she shrugged. Traitor.

"That was nothing." I let out a sigh as I floated on my back.

"That was definitely something," Chiara insisted. "Orlando hadn't paid attention to a woman in years."

"He's being kind," I argued. "Girls, I should be relaxing. Another relationship is the last thing I have on my mind."

"Who said anything about a relationship?" Skyler laughed. "You can flirt. He's the perfect distraction."

"That's not healthy advice," Chiara said. "She should do whatever she wants to do."

"Sometimes people need a push to go after what they want," Rosie commented. "I'd say keep an open mind, take what comes your way, and leave what doesn't."

"What does that mean?" I asked as I waded through the water.

"Exactly what I said." Rosie shrugged. "Just remember my mantra when the opportunity presents itself."

"Live at the moment. Yeah, I know that," I said mockingly before taking a dip and letting the water consume me for a moment. It was so peaceful under the water.

"Come on, we've been in the sun for too long. Let's chill out." Chiara beckoned when I surfaced.

The men were already out of the water and had pulled the chairs in a semi-circle with umbrellas to give us a cover from the sun. The table was moved to the center, and I noticed a new table that now held sandwiches and fresh juices.

I took off my wet trousers and occupied an empty chair before grabbing my phone. Snapping a photo of the refreshments, I posted it on Instagram before checking out the notifications. There were many hearts and snide comments from Alana's bitches, which I ignored. *There will always be haters.*

Then a certain comment caught my attention.

CortezO: That's encouraging.

The tips of my ears heated, and in my peripheral vision, I noticed Orlando coming to sit beside me. It almost slipped my mind that we followed each other on Instagram. I fought the urge to hide my face in my hands.

Our friends were giving us knowing smirks, and before I knew it, my phone beeped with notifications. They were commenting one after the other.

My phone beeped again, showing a new message on Instagram. *This bikini suits you well.* I wanted to die of embarrassment. Beside me, Orlando browsed through his phone as if he hadn't messaged me at all.

I typed a response before putting my phone aside. This day was turning out better than I expected.

Chapter 8

When Mike invited me for a round on the jet ski, I declined with a polite smile. I didn't know why I felt uneasy all of a sudden. It looked fun, but I didn't feel like riding. I watched and took pictures from the shore as my friends enjoyed their day. I was content with the distraction that often paraded shirtless along the beach.

The change in the atmosphere and the sea's exceptional calming effect kept my mind in check. For the first time, I wasn't pulled deep into the depressing memories of the person I tried hard to forget.

When everyone returned to the shore, I stood and pulled on my now dry trousers.

"The sun will set soon. Let's ride the jet ski and meet back at the yacht for dinner," Enrique suggested, and everyone agreed except me. I thought we would get ready for the evening and then walk. The pier was just about fifteen-to-twenty minutes' walk from here. On the jet ski, you had to go around the small island to get there.

"Orlando, hope you don't mind taking Ari with you," Mike yelled as he dragged Skyler to his jet ski.

I watched in horror as all the couples left me without a second thought, and now I was stuck with Orlando.

"You don't have to..." My voice wavered as I admired my toes, my breathing erratic. "I don't want to be a trouble." I couldn't tell him the thought of being out on the sea unsettled my stomach. I had never been in the ocean before.

"You're no trouble." His tone was clipped as he turned and walked to his jet ski.

I took it as my cue to follow him. Climbing on wasn't hard, but there was no place I could hold on to. My eyes darted to the vast ocean as my mind supplied all the worst possible scenarios. Fear crept up my spine. Looking at it from a distance was one thing, but being out there, surrounded by nothing but the water, was unnerving.

"You'll have to hold me if you don't want to fall off."

I barely had time to register his words when the engine powered up, and I jerked forward, holding onto him with all the strength I had. When we shot forward, I was breathless, literally.

Everything was a blur, and I didn't know what was happening. Suddenly, the spinning stopped, and Orlando shook me.

"Stop screaming! We're not moving."

It wasn't until he told me that I realized I was screaming. My mouth shut, and when I looked around, I lost it.

"Oh, God! No, no, no, no, no."

I began breathing through my mouth.

"Take me back!"

My panic rose.

"Take me back."

Water surrounded us.

Deep and taunting.

"Oh, God! This is..."

I saw nothing but blue.

"Orlando..."

"Relax, Arianna."

"Please take me back." Somehow, the sight was suffocating me. I decided the sea was not for me. I couldn't explain my fear to him. Being out here made me so vulnerable, though, to what I didn't know. I felt helpless, and I didn't like it.

"Okay. We can go back once you've settled down."

Orlando's voice was calm and controlled. My friends were nowhere in sight.

"I'm calm," I lied, all the while trembling inside. My hold on Orlando hadn't relaxed.

"I'm going to turn around, and we're going to go back, okay?"

"Okay."

I felt his chest expand under the tight grip of my arms before he powered up the engine.

"Wait!"

"Now what?" he snapped.

"I'll sit in front."

"You want to drive?"

"No. It's just...I'm scared." I hesitated before voicing my fear. I didn't know if I could handle the trip back, and I'd already embarrassed myself.

Orlando seemed to contemplate my words before he pried my hands off him, only for me to tighten again. "You do realize that you can only move if you let go of me, right?" His voice held a tint of amusement. "I suggest you close your eyes."

I obeyed immediately. I wanted to smack my head as I loosened my grip and allowed him to guide me to the front, my eyes closed all the while. Orlando practically lifted me up and settled me down in front of him.

"Can we go now?" he asked.

My position was uncomfortable at best. I sat facing him, and the handlebar was behind me. It was awkward, but it was also a welcomed distraction from the view of the sea.

"Why aren't you wearing a life jacket?"

"I don't need one."

"What if you fall?"

He ignored my question. "Why did you come if you're afraid of the water?"

"I'm not usually afraid. Being out here in the open makes me uneasy."

His gray eyes assessed me for a moment. "Now that your position is changed, do you think we can go for a round?"

"I don't know."

"Hold on to me. If you aren't comfortable, then we head back to shore, okay?"

I cast a nervous look around before meeting his gaze again. "Okay." My cheeks heated up as I noticed his naked torso. *So close.*

It was a task to hold him without showing my discomfort or embarrassment. Fortunately, he didn't comment. When we moved again, my legs came up, hooking around his waist, and my arms tightened their hold as I buried my face into his neck.

The water, the sound of the engine running, or the bounces it caused never mattered as I focused on not blushing. Being so close to Orlando made my insides flutter.

A feeling somewhere between sinful and uncomfortable crept in. Sinful because a part of me enjoyed the closeness. Uncomfortable because I'd never been so close to him before.

When my eyes opened a few minutes later, my insides were calm. But a new fear made my body tremble as I saw the island growing smaller in the distance.

"Orlando...we are...oh, God!"

As if on cue, the engine sputtered before shutting off.

"What's happening?" My panic rose.

"I forgot to check the fuel tank."

"What? You forgot to check your fuel tank?"

His serious expression didn't change even after a minute. Large hands cupped my face and stopped me from turning around.

"Don't look."

"I...I..." I couldn't help the panic. Even though he stopped me from looking around, I could still see behind, and it wasn't helping my situation. Water was everywhere. I shouldn't have agreed to come here.

"Arianna..." he said, "look at me."

When I looked at him, I couldn't help but admire his chiseled face inches from mine. Butterflies fluttered in my lower belly. *Oh, uh.* What the hell was happening? It must be the sea.

"I don't want to die yet," I squeaked. Not what I meant to say, but it was the truth.

"You won't."

While his hands stopped me from turning, there was no stopping my eyes from taking a stroll. That was enough. But before I panicked, I saw Orlando's face coming closer.

A warm tingle ignited as soon as our lips connected. *Orlando Cortez is kissing me.* A gasp of disbelief was all he needed to deepen the kiss. Oh, boy, was he a good kisser.

His tongue swept against mine briefly, and I was too shocked to respond. Just as it started, it finished. I blinked to clear my hazy vision. I realized I was doing that a lot these days.

"Turn around."

"Huh?"

"Unhook your legs from my waist."

"Oh." I didn't know if my cheeks could get any hotter as I untangled my legs from his narrow, muscular waist.

"Stand up and keep your eyes on me."

My body behaved as if it was on autopilot as I did as I was told. In an instant, I sat facing the ocean, and I couldn't take my eyes off the sight before me.

Orange sky greeted me above the blue sea. The sun was about to set, and I basked in the golden glow. I'd never seen a sunset this close. We had an excellent view here with no disruptions of buildings or people.

My brain registered the peaceful silence around us. The only sound was the slight tapping of water on the ski as the gentle wind brushed my skin.

"It's so beautiful," I whispered as I watched the sea slowly swallow the fireball.

"It is."

His hot breath on my right ear made me jump slightly, but my eyes weren't on the sunset anymore. When I turned, our eyes locked. There was an unreadable expression on his face as he lowered his head.

***

Neither of us spoke about the kiss again, and everything went back to normal. Orlando lied about the fuel in our jet ski. It had been a day since our kiss, and that was all I could think about that night as I lay on my bed.

"Ari, can you hand me that brush?"

Rosie's voice distracted me from my thoughts. I obeyed silently as Rosie worked on my hair. I was certainly not looking forward to the event this evening. "Should we really be going to this thing? I thought it's only for their business associates."

Rosie chuckled under her breath. "You agreed to be Orlando's date, remember? He said he'll be here to accompany you shortly."

I snorted, not amused by the idea. "If this is anything like the parties at my parents', I'll be back in my room in no time." Orlando could manage alone.

"That's up to you."

There was a knock at the door. "He's here." Rosie went to open the door, and I followed. All I wanted to do now was to stay in and watch a movie or two.

"You look gorgeous." An appreciative tone brought me out of my sulking thoughts. My eyes snapped to Orlando, who appeared as handsome as ever in his gray suit.

"Thank you." My smile couldn't be helped as I looped my hand in his elbow. The self-consciousness I normally felt around Brian was absent when I was with Orlando. My shoulders straightened, and my strides grew more confident with every step I took.

"Thanks for joining me, Arianna," Orlando said softly as we drew closer. "I'm not really looking forward to this, but being a host, I can't skip the event."

"No problem." Though I wasn't looking forward to staying, I decided to try for Orlando's sake.

Chapter 9

I stifled my yawn and focused on the brunette who was making my ears bleed. She was going on about all the designer brands that were in her closet and the number of fashion shows she had hosted in her career. The worst part was she recognized me as a Swanson and didn't miss a chance to sing my parents' praise.

"If you don't mind, Ms. Weston, I promised my girl a dance." Orlando arrived to rescue me. The woman's mouth went slack as I graciously accepted his hand with a sigh of relief. "Sorry for that. I got caught in a conversation and couldn't get away," he said as he led me to the dance floor.

"This party is boring as fuck."

Orlando's brows rose in question before he chuckled under his breath. "Don't say that too loud. I'm their host, remember?" he casually joked as we moved around the dance floor.

I couldn't help but compare him with Brian at times like this. Brian would get offended and didn't appreciate my cussing. Had it been him, he'd have lectured me for an hour, unlike Orlando, who didn't care.

Our feet moved in a practiced rhythm. I still wondered why everyone fancied waltzes for a business meeting. It was slow and romantic, while the event had nothing to do with romance. Most of the business associates were drinking and chatting, all looking bored to death.

"Orlando..."

"Mhmm."

"Can we leave yet? I'd rather be in my room and do nothing."

He thought about it for a moment and looked around. Enrique and Chiara moved lazily beside us. When Orlando's eyes met mine again, he grinned. The first real smile he'd ever given me. "I think we can. Enrique and Dad can manage."

Soon, we were both heading toward our rooms. I removed my heels and picked them up, enjoying how the cold marble felt against my bare feet. "Thanks for doing this."

"It's nothing." He shrugged off his coat and loosened his tie.

When we reached my room, he paused. "Um...do you want to hang out for a while?" I asked, my voice hesitant at first. "I'm gonna watch a movie or two."

"Sure," Orlando said. "As long as you don't force me to watch something sad, I'm in."

I opened the door wide for him to enter and walked to the closet. "I need to change," I called over my shoulder. Removing the tight dress was liberating. I couldn't wait to get into my comfy pajama shorts and a t-shirt.

***

"Mike told me about your parents. Where they always like this?" Orlando asked me out of the blue.

I was so used to my parents' attitude that I had forgotten the last time they were good to me. "They weren't affectionate. They expected us to follow their path, and I, for one, was never good with their rules."

I was often grounded and scolded for unknown reasons. "The day after my seventeenth birthday, I came home late after my party. They were waiting for me in the living room."

My eyes stung as the memories surfaced.

"They said they were ashamed of me. Mom slapped me and called me a slut. 'I can't believe my daughter is a slut,' were her exact words. Dad asked me to leave and never come back. Then Grandma stopped them, saying if the media got wind of this, it would ruin their reputation."

"What happened at the party?"

"It was wild, like any other party. I got drunk. Mike locked me and Rosalinda in a room for the rest of the night." I cringed at the memory. "Dad showed me a newspaper that had printed photos of the party. I think that's what set them off."

"So, they stopped talking to you?"

"Yeah, and they froze my funds."

"What about your college?"

"I got a scholarship and took part-time jobs to manage the expenses. I moved in with Rosalinda and Mike after a few months, and they also helped."

Mike's parents had bought him a condo near our university. We moved in together shortly after, and our college life was pure bliss. I realized I had suffered little since my friends supported me.

"How do you handle it? I mean, your ex and your sister, knowing they're sleeping together. It hurts more than anyone can imagine, doesn't it?"

"It does," I admitted. "A lot since she's my twin, and she knew we were together. Fortunately, I never slept with him. It made things easier, in a way."

"What? You were dating for—"

"Five months. I wanted to wait, and Brian was always keen on keeping our relationship under wraps. It didn't sit well with me. I wanted people to know that we are seeing each other."

"What an asshole."

"I know, right?" I chuckled as I moved closer to him. "Do you mind?" I asked as I leaned on his shoulder, inhaling his intoxicating cologne.

"No."

"Thanks. I need this now." I exhaled, looped my hand around his arm, and relaxed. "Why don't you talk about it?"

"About what?"

"About your past." I wanted to know. Well, he'd asked about mine. I felt his body tense before he responded.

"I don't have anything to tell." His voice was gruff and void of emotion. His shoulders had gone stiff, and it only confirmed my theory.

"Okay, if you say so." I didn't want to push him further. Maybe his scars ran deeper than mine.

I felt him relax after a few minutes.

"I'm sorry," he whispered. "I don't like to talk about my past."

"It's okay." I sighed. "Tell me when you're ready."

"Okay."

We fell into a comfortable silence and watched the movie until I could no longer keep my eyes open.

***

"What are our plans for today?" Rosie asked no one in particular as we finished our breakfast on the patio overlooking the sea.

"We'll go swimming and camping. Arrangements are already made, and four tents are being built as we speak," Mike said.

"What?" I squeaked. "I never knew you could go camping here."

"That's because you were here only twice, and the weather wasn't favorable," Mike countered. "Pack a swimsuit."

A few hours later, we were lounging in a clearing with a man-made pond as the men set up the tents. "Hey, where do I sleep? You guys forgot my tent," I yelled to the men. I gave a stink eye to the girls, who giggled in response.

"Didn't Rosie tell you? You're sharing the tent with Orlando," Mike called in response, and I noticed Orlando shaking his head with a small smile.

"This is not a joke," I hissed before plopping down between Rosie and Chiara. "You didn't have to out me like that."

"We didn't," Rosie protested. "It's logical. We're here for a vacation, and we sure wouldn't want to spend time away from our men, would we? And Mike thought it would be safer for you to share a tent with Orlando. It isn't like you guys aren't sleeping together. Ouch!" Rosie hissed and rubbed the area where I'd just pinched her.

"We aren't sleeping together!"

"I didn't mean it that way, bish. Chill!"

"How did you mean it, then?"

"Well, I saw you sleeping together in your room last night. You did sleep together, didn't you?"

I groaned. "Stop putting it that way. We fell asleep together."

"Same thing." She shrugged, and I gave up. There was no point in arguing with her. They decided to hook me up with Orlando, and there was no stopping them now.

"Did you check your Instagram today?" Skyler asked.

"No. Did I miss something?" I was so caught up with everything around me, and since everyone I was usually in touch with was here with me, I actually didn't give a thought to checking my phone. Suddenly, I wanted to check my profile to see if there were any new comments on Orlando's photo.

"I won't say you particularly missed it," Chiara drawled. "Your twin-bitch has shared a few candid moments with a hashtag 'throw back.'"

I was quick to pull my phone from my overnight bag and open the app. The photos were indeed candid moments, but they also revealed so many things I didn't know. It didn't take long for me to recognize Alana's gown from a themed party that was held exactly four months ago. Brian and Alana appeared cozy in our garden. I had left the party after half an hour and didn't know Brian had attended it *until now.*

"I dodged a bullet, didn't I?" I refused to break down again. Brian was seeing Alana behind my back. Or was he seeing me behind her back? My mind raced.

"You did, and I can't believe that bastard fooled all of us."

"Our parents are business partners. It only makes sense when they've known each other for so long." My voice lowered to a whisper as memories raged in my mind. I never visited my father's office. Alana would often go to work with him when she had nothing else to do. "He bluffed when he said meeting me was an accident," I said when no one spoke.

Now, there were questions creeping into my mind. *What was Brian's motive?*

"Are you thinking what I'm thinking?" Rosie balanced herself on her elbows.

"I want to know what Brian's motive was. Why would he lie when they were already seeing each other?"

"Hmm…maybe some sick and twisted plan of your sister dearest to get her revenge," Chiara said.

"Revenge for what? I moved out at seventeen. I only moved back in two months ago, and that was because Mike sold his condo, and I was looking for a decent place to stay."

It didn't make sense. I moved in mere days before Brian proposed to Alana. My parents weren't thrilled. But I had resigned from my job and thought it wasn't a good idea to invest my hard-earned money in a home before I had another job. Alana had free rein over our father's funds, and she made it her business to poke her nose into my business. For example, inviting me over for a family dinner every Sunday was her idea.

In the eyes of my parents, she was playing a perfect daughter, trying to bring the family together, while all she did was degrade me. Though I didn't want to be a part of their lives, I went to the dinners and parties simply to remind them I was their daughter too. Perhaps a little part of me longed for their approval. However, I was sure of one thing. Brian wasn't honest when I confronted him. *What was he even thinking?*

While I wanted to know the answers, another thought crossed my mind. *Does it matter?*

"Hey!" I yelled in surprise when Mike took my phone.

"I'll throw this in the pond if you keep looking at that."

"I wasn't looking."

"No. You were thinking, trying to find answers for questions that don't matter anymore."

A deep sigh left my lips, and I raised my arms in surrender. "I won't sulk, promise."

He handed me the phone with a smirk. "Good. Put this to good use like yesterday. I'll pose for you if you want."

I snorted. "Drooling over you is her job now." I pointed at Skyler, who snickered at my comment. "I'll stick with my date for now."

Mike shrugged with a cheeky grin. "Can't complain." When he turned, he did what he always did—pull the rug from under me. "Hey, Orlando!" he hollered. "Mind posing for this chick here?"

I groaned when Orlando walked toward us with a smug grin. "What would you prefer, Arianna? Front or back?" His voice dripped with a fake sweetness that made me narrow my eyes at him.

Orlando – 1; Arianna – 0

"Well, how about a nude one?"

Orlando – 0; Arianna – 1

My friends chuckled under their breath as Orlando shook his head with a full-blown smile. I shrugged, feeling happy because I got even with him. It was now my turn to smirk, and I did so, taking a swig of water from my bottle.

"As long as you're the only one who would see it, I don't mind."

The next thing I knew, the water I was drinking had entered my nostrils, and I was choking as everyone burst into laughter.

Orlando – 1; Arianna – 0

"Are you okay?" Orlando's concerned face loomed over me as the others clutched their stomachs, unable to control their laughter.

Not trusting my words, I raised both my thumbs at him and nodded with what must have been a constipated-looking smile. This day couldn't get any better.

Chapter 10

Rosie caught up with me just as I exited the pond, throwing a towel at me. "I have something for them to mull over," she said and winked.

"What did you do now?" I knew immediately she had posted something on Instagram.

Rosie giggled as she swiped her thumb across the screen. My breath hitched as soon as the post came into view. The sudden rush of blood to my brain drowned all the sounds around me. I recognized the moment she'd captured, and the memory warmed my heart.

Orlando had his hands around my waist as a pristine smile adorned his lips. My orange gown with gold embroidery contrasted well with his gray suit. It was his first real smile in a long time. My eyes were mesmerized as I looked at him, and the camera had captured it all.

"When did you take this?"

"Oh, I was passing by and saw two birds picking sticks to build their nest. Couldn't help but capture what I thought would be one of the many best moments to come."

Goose bumps erupted on my flesh as my eyes widened. "Rosie..." My voice was barely a whisper.

"It's too early, I know. But I can't deny it, Ari. I feel it when you two are together. I see it in your eyes—both of your eyes. I see the joy in yours and hope in his. I have this gut feeling that says you're meant for each other."

She sounded sincere, and I believed her. It sounded too good. When my eyes found Orlando, with Mike in a choke hold, sporting a huge grin on his face, hope bloomed in my heart. I didn't know what to do about it.

"I see how much he's changed, Ari. He just hasn't realized it yet," Rosie's soft voice continued. "He's laughing and talking a lot. He's coming out of his shell."

Rosie's words kept replaying in my mind as I went to lie under the canopy of a tree. My eyes once again went to Orlando. I took the phone and recorded the guys laughing out loud and bickering with each other. It had been too long since I saw them together like this, almost ten years.

A beep distracted me, and a frown crept onto my face when I noticed a text.

Brian: What are you trying to prove? Do you realize how much stress this puts on your parents?

What was the matter with this guy? Why did he think he had the right to message me now? Fury bubbled within the cavity of my chest.

Brian: I'm ashamed of you, Arianna. I thought you'd be better, but you proved again how low you'd go to disgrace your family.

What was he talking about? Now I was really confused. His message didn't make sense. If he meant my Instagram posts, I didn't feel like there was anything wrong about it. I typed, "Who do you think you are?" Then I recalled what Mike and Rosie had told me. To move on, I had to forget and distract myself. No matter how hard it was, I forced myself to ignore the message and deleted it so I wouldn't go back to check and respond. His words, however, kept replaying in the back of my mind. What was he implying? Why would he say he thought I'd be better, and I proved him wrong? What did I do?

***

"Truth or dare!"

I groaned at Mike's announcement. His version of truth or dare had always been embarrassing. Mike took the game too seriously and always made sure the participants fulfilled the conditions. While I was thinking about an excuse, I noticed everyone gathering on the ground, forming a circle. There went my chance.

"Ari! Aren't you coming?" Rosie hollered.

"Nope. I'm gonna lay down for a while."

"Two minutes before I come and drag your ass here," Mike, Satan in disguise, called.

"I'm coming."

Orlando and Jeff, who were unaware of how Mike's game usually ended, sat there, clueless.

"Should I be concerned?" Orlando asked when I went to sit beside him. "Your face tells me you don't have a good experience with his games."

"Too late." I sighed. "Friendly advice: stick to the truth."

Orlando nodded as Mike started with a mischievous grin. He had set a small stool in the middle with an empty beer bottle on it. I looked at the sky, praying Mike would let me walk out of this place with dignity.

"Enrique!"

The crowd cheered.

"Truth or dare?" Mike asked.

"Dare." Enrique smirked.

Clever. I knew him enough to know he'd never choose the truth. Once he did, and that day, I learned how many women he'd slept with and how often he masturbated in a week. Yep, Mike is an asshole with all capitals with this game.

"I knew you'd choose a dare, pal," Mike drawled. "Hence, I crafted something special for you. Wear this until the game ends."

When Mike pulled a leafy thing from behind his back, everyone burst into laughter, including me.

Enrique held it in his hand, and his nose scrunched. "Is this a joke? How do I even wear it?" He unfolded the delicate looking skirt made of only leaves.

"Can we switch it for a kerchief instead?'

"Nope. You know the rules." Mike shrugged. "And, no briefs, buddy."

I felt Orlando stiffen beside me, and I threw him an I-told-you-so look.

We burst into laughter when Enrique came out wearing it, or more accurately, holding it in one hand and covering his crotch using the other.

"Mother Nature would be so proud of you." Mike clapped and rotated the bottle for the next round.

After Enrique's turn, everyone mostly chose the truth, fearing what Mike would make them do. Enrique knelt, resting his ass on his heels because sitting in any other position without flashing us was impossible.

"How many women have you had sex with?"

Jeff coughed and looked at Rosie with wide eyes. Rosie shrugged.

"I'll choose dare." Jeff shifted uncomfortably.

"You can't change it, Jeff." The devious grin on his face would look perfect with a pair of demon ears and a spiked tail.

"I don't know," Jeff answered with a resigned sigh.

"What's your number, mate?" Enrique teased.

Jeff's pleading eyes met Rosie's, and I felt pity for the guy. "Twenty-something. I'm sorry, babe. But it was during my college days. I'm not the same person anymore."

Twenty. Wow.

Suddenly, I was curious about Orlando's turn. What would he say?

"It's okay, Jeff. That was in the past." Rosie shrugged and patted his shoulder. Jeff visibly relaxed and pulled her into his embrace before kissing the crown of her head.

My heart sped up when it was Orlando's turn. "How many girls have you slept with?" Mike asked as if reading my mind.

Orlando stiffened but then relaxed. "One."

I released the breath I didn't realize I was holding. What did I expect?

"Arianna," Mike pulled me out of my thoughts, "your turn. Who was your first crush?" I cursed, throwing a furious glare at him. His grin widened as he urged me to answer. "Remember, I already know the answer," he warned.

Beside me, Orlando was looking at me, his expression unreadable.

I took a deep breath. I should've known this was coming. "Orlando." My whisper was barely audible.

"We didn't hear it. Louder, please..." Mike chuckled.

Asshole. He did this on purpose. "Orlando Gabriele Cortez," I said through my gritted teeth as my cheeks heated. There was no way I could face Orlando now. Crap!

I was the first person to run to the tent when the game was over. I didn't know which was more embarrassing, answering the question about my crush or when he asked me who I would've chosen to lose my V-card to, Brian or Orlando. "Somebody kill me now," I groaned as I buried my face into the pillow. I was an idiot. I should've chosen a dare after the first question.

A soft chuckle made me sit up. Ah, here came my fourth embarrassment of the day. I didn't dare meet Orlando's gaze. My dignity clung to me by a thread, and I was sure by the end of the day, it would be dead and gone.

"There's nothing to be embarrassed about, you know," Orlando said calmly, and I covered my face again.

"I hate Mike."

Orlando chuckled again. "Thanks for the friendly advice, by the way." He was getting comfortable in the tent, and instead of leaving like I expected him to, he just lay there.

"And look where it got me. I should've known better."

"Would you prefer masturbating underwater while sounding as if you're in a porn movie?"

I grimaced. That was what Enrique got in his second round of dare. I had to close my ears and eyes during the session. The men were laughing, and Chiara was beet red when I opened my eyes again. Skyler, like me, had closed her eyes and ears while Jeff covered Rosie's eyes.

"Nope."

"You got nothing to worry about. It's just me."

I didn't know what to think anymore. But I didn't respond to Orlando.

When night came, everyone settled in their tents with their men. I lay there with Orlando, pretending to sleep. Being alone with him in the same tent after revealing I had a crush on him was the most awkward moment I'd ever had.

Fortunately, Orlando didn't comment, and I was thankful. My peace didn't last long as sounds began coming from a nearby tent. My ears heated up when I realized what it was. Moans and grunts threw stones at my peace, adding more to my embarrassment. If that wasn't enough, more sounds started from the second tent and then the third.

My eyes widened as I sat straight. What the hell were they doing?

Beside me, Orlando cleared his throat. "That's unwarranted."

"They're doing it on purpose, I swear," I hissed as I covered my ears.

It now sounded as if they were competing with each other on who screamed louder. Again, I shouldn't be surprised since everyone except Orlando and me was drunk.

"I'm going out for a walk." Orlando stood.

"Wait, I'm coming with you."

We almost ran out of the place like bats out of hell, and I relaxed when we were out of hearing range.

"Why don't you drink?" I asked as Orlando sat on a rock beside the pond. Moonlight illuminated the surroundings, making it look like a place out of a fairy tale.

"I drink beer."

"You know what I meant. Besides, you refused the beer today." I sat beside him and threw the blanket around his shoulders before closing the distance between us and settling against him.

"That's because I knew I'd be sharing the tent with you. Also, at least one person has to be sober at night when everyone else is wasted."

I nodded. "And you don't drink much otherwise because...?"

"Because there are things I don't want to forget." His answer was terse, body stiff.

"Sounds reasonable." I looked away at the pond as I leaned my head on his shoulder. "Let's talk about something else. What's your favorite color?"

"Purple and blue. What's yours?"

"Red and black. What movies do you prefer?"

"Comedy."

"No way. Me too."

Soon, I ran out of questions and asked him, "What was the most embarrassing thing you did when you were younger?"

Orlando chuckled. "I lost a bet and had to twerk in front of the class while wearing high heels. Worst of all, someone shot it and posted on Facebook. It went viral, and they didn't let me forget."

I laughed, imagining how he'd have looked. "I want to see that someday."

"No, you don't."

I just laughed in response.

"What about you?" he asked.

"Ah, you don't want to know."

"I told you mine."

"Well, let's say I still live it."

"What did you do?" he asked.

"I told you about my wild birthday party, right?" Orlando nodded. "Well, we had hired a tattoo artist, a DJ, and a few strippers too."

Orlando's eyes widened, and he masked the laughter with a cough.

"We played truth or dare, and with my drunken courage, I chose dare."

"What did he do?" Orlando sported an amused smile as his eyes bore into mine.

"I ended up getting a tattoo on my ass."

Orlando boomed with laughter. "Do I even want to know what it is?"

"No." I shook my head. *You'll find out soon enough.* My sudden thought shocked me and made my cheeks burn.

"So, what's on it?"

"You'll have to see for yourself." I bit the inside of my cheeks and averted my gaze when I realized I had said it out loud.

"Is that an invitation?" His brows quirked as a smile spread on his lips.

My mind was like a lost needle in a haystack as I gazed into his eyes. "Do you think they would be done by now?" I changed the topic, not trusting myself anymore. *He is too hot for his own good.*

Orlando shrugged. The moment of heat simmered as we gazed at the pond. "We should head back and check. Or you can stay here while I take a quick look," he suggested.

"I'll wait here." My answer came without hesitation. I watched him go and turned my attention to the pond. I'd rather sit here in the dark wondering about the ghosts that roamed at night rather than hear their sounds of pleasure.

"It's clear," Orlando announced and helped me up. Together, we headed to our tent.

Chapter 11

Silence.

So comfortable.

A gentle breeze ruffled the material of the tent as I tried to sleep. My heart fluttered and did a somersault thinking about being so close to Orlando again. I fell asleep with him twice before, but this confined space felt too intimate.

My body stiffened when I felt him move. I hadn't changed my position, pretending to sleep. A few excruciating seconds later, I felt his hand snaking around my waist and pulling me closer.

"Good night, Arianna," he whispered.

A gasp escaped my lips as my belly dipped. He continued to bury his face in my hair, and his sigh of contentment brushed my skin. I should've pretended to be asleep and slept like that, but I couldn't help the grin that lit my face.

I turned around in his arms and pressed my cheek against his warm chest, realizing he had removed his shirt before lying down. "What a loser," I mumbled and snuggled closer.

"Huh?" Orlando said hesitantly.

"I said she's a loser," I repeated and felt his heart racing. That was a good sign. My grin widened. It showed I affected him too.

"Who's a loser?"

"The one who let you slip through her fingers," I clarified and felt him stiffen in my arms. "It's her loss and my gain." I tightened my hold on him and wondered for a moment if he'd push me away.

He didn't, and instead, his body relaxed. "I thought you were asleep."

"I couldn't sleep." I paused, then added, "Brian messaged me today." Orlando once again stiffened. "He said I was putting an unwanted stress on my parents. That I proved again that I was a disgrace to my family."

"Have you responded?" I felt his stress, though his voice was void of emotions.

"No. I deleted his message. Whatever we had, it was over, and I want none of this. Maybe he's trying to exert his powers as my brother-in-law, you know, trying to lecture me and all."

"Good," Orlando murmured, and his hold around me tightened. A relieved breath hit the crown of my head as I brought myself as close to him as possible. I wanted him to say more, but he didn't.

"Good night, Orlando."

"Good night, Arianna."

***

When we woke the next morning, there was an ease in his smile. It was like we had been together much longer than we had. It was true; we had known each other for years. Mike always told us about his family and about Orlando, and I was sure he did the same with Orlando, talking about his friends.

However, this was the first time Orlando and I got to spend so much time together. The first time, we were more than a cousin's friend and friend's cousin. I didn't stop to wonder where this would lead us. We were comfortable with what we had, and we didn't need to discuss it.

We enjoyed breakfast by the pit fire, and when it was time to pack, I joined Orlando. I had to admit I enjoyed the hangover look everyone sported this morning. It served them right for acting like cats in heat last night.

"There's a British-themed costume party tonight, if you don't know already," Orlando announced as we packed the tent.

"What?" An involuntary groan left my lips as I looked at him. "We just had a party."

"That was for business associates. This one is for Enrique and Chiara's friends."

"Ugh! Can I be excused?"

"Nope," he shook his head, "you're my date, remember?"

"And what am I dressing as?"

"An eighteenth-century maiden." Orlando's smile only widened when he noticed the appalled look on my face. *He is kidding, right?*

"I'd prefer to go as a hooker."

"We're talking about the eighteenth century, hon. You'd still be required to dress to please."

That's it. I'm packing and leaving this Godforsaken party this instant.

"You're not leaving," Orlando commented as he suppressed a laugh. I could tell my face was a dead giveaway of what was on my mind. "I'll be at your door at seven p.m." With that, he lifted the folded tent with ease, carrying it to the Jeep.

"You look constipated," Rosie chirped as she nudged my ribs.

"Did you hear what he said?"

"About the costume party, right?" Her face lit up. "I'm so excited. It's going to be fun."

I palmed my face, cursing myself for even asking her. *Party freak.* A permanent scowl had replaced my otherwise calm expression as I climbed into my seat. Should I feign illness? Orlando wouldn't believe me. Then, a sudden idea clicked. I'd tell them I got my period. Yes!

"Don't even think about it," Rosie deadpanned beside me as if reading my thoughts. "You finished your period three days ago."

Orlando's chest rumbled with laughter in the front seat. A deep, rich sound I'd grown addicted to. *Bitch!*

Rosie shrugged off the death glares I gave her. This, right here, was the con of friends you'd known since kindergarten. They knew exactly how your mind worked.

***

My scowl deepened, and my hatred toward the costume party rose to a new level as the assistant they hired for the party secured the knots of my corset. If possible, my eyes almost bulged out of my head when she pulled the last thread. My generous breasts were now flat, pulled tightly against my body.

The painstaking process of dressing consumed a solid thirty minutes. I continued to take shallow breaths as the dress limited the movement of my lungs. Fuck! I hated this. Never in my life had I worn so much clothing at one time. The corset, petticoats, additional hidden pockets, a roll, stockings, garters, the gown, a stomacher, a kerchief, an apron, shoes, and complicated layers of clothing. I didn't even know the name of most of my garments until the assistant calmly explained what they were.

All the knowledge gained went down the drain when the simpler task of breathing became the main focus. I wondered how women moved around in these things. The weight and length of the garment seemed to pull me down. I couldn't even sit without feeling the bamboo thing she added around my waist that made my skirt flare. The low-cut neck did nothing to improve my breathing.

I'd gladly kill Orlando right this moment if he showed his face. Rosalinda, the traitor, trotted like an elegant feline, twirling around and admiring her outfit while I resembled a grumpy cat. Fortunately, everyone agreed on not using those funny-looking wigs. Our hair was curled and pinned to our head, leaving loose strands to rest on our shoulders.

I turned and hissed like a possessed woman when a knock sounded exactly at seven p.m. A string of profanities got stuck in my throat as Orlando's striking features caught me off guard. He was extremely sexy in his outfit and looked every bit a British lord.

"Shall we?"

Stop it, Arianna. You should be killing him now. I tried to remember my anger when he gave me a dashing smile. *I'll kill him later.* I focused on walking and not falling.

I managed to reach the party hall without tripping and finally looked up. My breath caught in my throat when I took note of the arrangements. The normally exquisite banquet hall was transformed into an eighteenth-century ballroom. The long curtains, tapestries, and paintings made me feel as if I was transported back in time.

"It's beautiful," I breathed. It was getting easier to breathe through the confines of my clothes. The younger crowd looked elegant in different colors of clothing and accessories. They appeared lively despite the soft orchestra playing in the background.

Though I initially despised the idea of a themed party, I found myself enjoying this one. Mainly because it didn't have any gossip mongers that often crowded my parents' parties. The guests were all couples in their mid-twenties through the early thirties. Several friendly smiles were thrown my way as we bumped into each other. My heart felt lighter as time passed.

Enrique and Chiara were the main focus. Dressed like a duke and duchess, they were the definition of a perfect couple, looking so much in love. Their joyful smiles were contagious. Orlando was attached to my side the entire time, taking me around and introducing me to his friends.

"Orlando, buddy, it's so good to see you." An excited voice greeted us as we made our way through the crowd. My eyes went wide when I noticed who it was. Dean McAllister played for the Green Bay Packers, one of the most popular teams in the National Football League.

"Dean!" Orlando's face lit up. "It's been a long time." The men hugged, clapping each other's backs before parting. "I can't believe you're here."

Dean McAllister is Orlando's friend? Wow!

"Enrique called." Dean grinned. "He even booked the tickets three months ago."

"It's good to see you, man. Thanks for coming."

Dean waved him off. "We should've gotten together earlier." His attention turned toward me, and I stood staring at him with my jaw ajar. "Is she with you?"

I blinked as his words registered. My gaze snapped to meet Orlando's, and our eyes locked, hope in mine and a smile in his. I saw no doubt in his eyes as his lips stretched, widening his smile.

"Yes, she is."

A silent gasp from me was the only response he got before I averted my face to hide my blush. Did he just call me his? He did. A secret smile graced my lips as butterflies fluttered in my belly.

"Congrats, man!" Dean was hugging Orlando again. "Congratulations, lady!" I tried to keep my blush at bay.

"Thanks." I couldn't hear my voice as my lips moved.

"Ari, can you hang out with Rosie and Skyler for a while? I'll be back soon," Orlando whispered in my ear. His eyes held a pleading look, and I understood his need to catch up with his old friend in private.

"Sure," I said. "You don't have to hurry."

"You're the best."

His soft peck on my cheek left me breathless, and I watched him lead Dean out of the party hall with a stunning smile.

"I saw that." I almost jumped out of my skin and whirled around to stare at Rosie, who laughed out loud.

"Rosie!" I hissed. "I told you not to do that."

"It's fun," she said happily. "Look." She waved her phone in front of my face.

It was a photo of Orlando pecking my cheek. "How did you even manage that?"

"I have my ways, just like you have yours." She winked.

I shook my head. "He called me his." I couldn't help but smile.

"I'm so happy for you, Ari. You deserve to be happy. When you stand at your twin bitch's wedding, I want you to smile wider. You won't cry for that jerk again."

Thinking about Brian didn't hurt as it did before. While it was too early to say where I stood with Orlando, I couldn't help but bask in the attention he was showering me with. He was everything Brian wasn't--simple truth. The more time I spent with Orlando, the more

I realized what I had with Brian wasn't what I'd have wanted in the long run. I'd have seen him for what he was and would've eventually left him. *Perhaps broken beyond repair.* I thanked my lucky stars now that it happened the way it had.

Chapter 12

"Hey, Rose, Jeff is looking for you," Mike said, his free arm slung over my shoulder as he nursed a fancy drink.

"Oh, I'll be right back."

"So, what's up, Ari?" Mike asked. "Or should I say, sister..."

"Mike..."

"I'm so happy for you, Ari." He kissed my forehead. "I know I warned you before, but I see how much Orlando has changed. Hoping for the best for you two."

"Thanks, Mike."

"Don't thank me yet. Look, I don't know what future holds, but I can tell he would never hurt you like Brian did. I know that much."

Before I could respond, the music stopped, and I saw Jeff climbing over a table. My eyes widened. *Oh, my God! This is it.* My phone. I patted down my hidden pockets, finding my phone in a hurry, not wanting to miss this beautiful moment. I'd been waiting for this for what felt like forever.

The crowd parted, clearing the path for Rosie as the lights dimmed. Two spotlights illuminated the couple as Jeff laughed nervously. Someone handed him a mic. "Rosalinda..." Jeff breathed. "I've been waiting for the right moment since last summer. Then I realized the time was always right, and I was a fool not to see it before."

I couldn't help the tears that stung my eyes—happy tears as I recorded everything.

"I'm one of the luckiest assholes in this world, literally. I was lost without you. I found my passion in you." Jeff climbed down the table and made his way to the sobbing mess that was my friend. "Rosalinda Pike, my speech sucks, so I'll stop right there and would like to ask the question that has been on my mind." He went down on his knee and produced the ring I helped him choose. "Will you make me the happiest man alive? Will you marry me?"

Rosie sobbed as she nodded vigorously. "Yes!" She jumped into his waiting arms and kissed him as he slipped the ring on her finger.

Tears now flowed freely down my cheeks as I recorded every moment. Suddenly, the scene changed in my mind's eye, and it was Brian who knelt instead of Jeff. It was Alana who kissed him instead of me. I sucked in a sharp breath and blinked away my tears. Everything was coming back, crashing down on me.

Crap! I thought I was over this shit.

I made my way quickly back toward my room. The clothes were once again suffocating me. I blindly swiped my phone, finding Orlando's number and calling him. *I need him.* Only Orlando seemed to chase away my demons.

"Arianna?"

"I need you, please..."

"I'm coming."

"Come to my room."

"Almost there."

I tripped several times in my attempt to get to the safety of my room while I clawed at my dress, trying to loosen the knots that pressed at my chest. Just as I entered my room, Orlando rushed in. My vision blurred as I gasped for breath, crawling on the floor. I felt like a fish out of water.

Orlando got down on his knees, working on my dress, cursing when he couldn't figure out which knot was where. It was all messed up. I saw him rush to the bathroom in my peripheral vision. When he returned, all I could hear for a while was the sound of clothes being ripped. He was cutting away the fabric and then used his hands to tear it.

Air rushed to my lungs, and I gulped greedily, gasping and breathing through my mouth. "Easy, there," Orlando murmured. "Keep breathing, Arianna. I'm here."

His hands now ran down my back, and I realized my top half was bare. I staggered to my feet, wanting to get rid of the clothing that still confined my lower half. "Please get it off."

"Okay, take it slow. It's okay. I'm here for you." Orlando caught me before I could trip again. Violent sobs wracked my body as he worked on the rest of my clothing.

"I hate him!" I cried. Cold air from the air conditioner brushed my bare skin as Orlando carefully lifted my feet, removing the remnants of the gown. "I hate that bastard."

"Shh..." Orlando cupped my face, his eyes boring into mine. "It's over now, Arianna."

I nodded as I concentrated on the gray of his eyes. "I let him do this to me." I cried more. "I hate the person I've become."

"You've become stronger, Arianna. You've become a better person."

"I don't feel like it." I shook my head. "One moment, I was happy for Rosie and Jeff. The next, all I could see and think about was him. The way he chose her. How he proposed to her."

Orlando was silent. His eyes scanned me. "We need to get you dressed. You're cold."

I wasn't. But my breath hitched when he turned away from me. Realization of what he would've seen dawned as my hands flew to my bare chest. I vaguely remember the assistant stopping me from wearing my bra and dressing me up in a cotton petticoat instead. *Oh, God!*

Orlando was searching my closet while I stood rooted to the floor. *Cover yourself with a blanket.* It was too late, though. Orlando was already walking toward me with my t-shirt in his hand and his eyes fixed on my face. No words were spoken when he helped me with the t-shirt. His eyes were on my face the entire time while I admired the marble floor.

I took the pajama bottoms from his hand silently and pulled them over the boxer panties I insisted on wearing that evening, secretly glad at least that was modest.

"I'll ask someone to bring dinner here." He went to the phone.

"I don't want anything," I whispered. Exhaustion washed over me, and I was emotionally drained. The evening started off well, and I found enjoying myself after a while. I never had panic attacks before. "Lay with me."

Orlando stopped, his face neutral. He shrugged off his coat and removed his tie and shoes before climbing into the bed. Without another word, I climbed beside him, resting my head on his chest. His one hand encircled my waist as the other pulled the blanket over us.

I snuggled further, letting my tears fall. I breathed in his cologne. "I'm sorry."

"For what?"

"For breaking down like that. I didn't know what to do," I confessed. "I thought I was over him. I wasn't expecting that Jeff proposing to Rosie would trigger me like that."

"It's okay to break down once in a while, Arianna. Pent-up emotions are more dangerous."

"Did you break down?"

"I did."

I wanted to ask more but decided against it. We were quiet for a while. I sighed contentedly when his fingers massaged my scalp, absentmindedly running through my hair. I couldn't help but compare Orlando and Brian again. How different they were. I tipped my head to see Orlando's eyes closed. Two of his shirt buttons were open, revealing his tan skin. His free hand rested on his chest.

"I never had panic attacks before. I ruined your time with Dean, didn't I?"

His eyes opened and focused on me. "No, you didn't." His knuckles brushed my cheek before pushing the loose strands out of my face. "I'm glad you called me when you did. You can call me anytime, Arianna. I promise to always be there for you."

"Don't make promises if you can't keep them."

"You know me better than that, Arianna. I don't make promises I don't intend to keep."

"I'm confused, Orlando. I like what's between us, but I'm too scared to talk about it."

"Then don't."

"What's your advice?"

"Just follow your heart." His voice was a few octaves lower.

Tears stung my eyes again. I wanted to kiss him right then. "Okay." My gaze went to his lips, lingering longer than it should. When I shifted my focus, I found him watching me intently. "I want to kiss you," I said, my voice husky.

"What's stopping you?" he asked.

"Don't know. Maybe it's because I'm afraid of rejection."

"I'll never reject you, Arianna. If you want to kiss me, then you should just do it."

His words were soothing, and once again, my lips stretched, forming a smile. I threw my leg over, climbing on top of him. When I closed the distance between our lips, I knew I wanted more. Orlando let me lead the kiss.

Soft and tentative at first.

My tongue darted out, tasting his firm lips. His mouth opened for me. He tasted like oranges. My hands pressed on his chest for balance as I adjusted my position. His hands encircled me, running over my back as his head rose to meet my lips.

This was nothing like when he kissed me the first time. I thought that was to distract me, and when he behaved as if nothing happened, I shrugged it off. But this was intense.

Consuming...

Claiming...

When he switched positions, I felt his growing hardness against my core. His hands held mine locked above my head. A soft moan escaped my lips when he rolled his hips. My legs spread wider, and my hip arched, trying to get him where I ached the most.

Orlando's lips left mine to pepper kisses along my jaw. When they met the soft spot on my neck, I panted. His teeth scraped my skin, nipping before sucking at the same spot. One of his hands climbed lower, resting just below the swell of my breast. My nipples hardened as they brushed against his chest. I wanted to get closer to him; it wasn't enough.

Then, abruptly, he stilled. "We should stop."

I blinked, trying to rein in my raging hormones. Why would he want to stop now? It felt good.

"I want you. But we should give it more time." Orlando was breathing harder.

"Okay." Disappointment clouded me, but his words made sense. I didn't want to be alone tonight. "Can you hold me?"

"Sure." He cleared his throat before lying beside me. I turned over, pressing my back to him. He held me like he did when we slept in our tent.

"Good night, Orlando."

"Good night, Arianna."

Chapter 13

A groan left my lips as I rolled over in bed. Morning hunger was gnawing at my insides, reminding me I had eaten nothing last night.

When I couldn't stand it any longer, I got up and went to the bathroom, quickly brushing my teeth. I washed my face and pulled my hair into a ponytail before I went downstairs. I was still in last night's clothes. My attire was presentable, and I didn't bother to change. The Cortezes had known me since I was a child, and this wasn't new.

"Good morning," I called to no one in particular and grabbed a piece of bacon from Mike's plate before taking a seat beside Orlando. Mike filled my plate while I grabbed another bite from his.

"What a tramp!"

My sleepy eyes snapped to the woman I hadn't seen before. *Did she just call me a tramp?* My eyes narrowed to slits as I swallowed the bacon.

"You call this thing your girlfriend? What a shame to the Cortez family," she continued as if I wasn't present.

"And who might you be?" I asked, oblivious to the tension in the room.

"You dare to question me, slut? What did you do to my son?"

Her son? However, before she could speak the next word, a voice boomed beside me.

"Enough!" Orlando's fist landed on the table. I jumped slightly and turned to see Orlando glaring at the woman. The glass of juice he held in his tight grip cracked at the impact, leaking its contents. "You'll not disrespect our guest. And you are not welcome here." All the remnants of sleep had left me now as my heart raced.

"Did you forget who I am?" the woman hissed, not fazed by his anger.

"Of course not." Orlando clenched his jaw. "I don't forget the ones who betrayed me, especially you."

"You—"

"Enough, Isabel!" Uncle Rick commanded. "Leave before we forcefully remove you from the property."

Oh, this must be the runaway mother Mike told us about.

"You can't do that, husband," the woman, Isabel, stressed in a sick-ly-sweet voice. Uncle Rick's face changed when she waved an envelope. "I have a court order."

"Not for long," Orlando snarled. His chest heaved as he stormed out of the room as the woman smirked. I'd never seen him this furious. I noticed his untouched plate and glared at the woman, who was now taking a seat beside Chiara. Uncle Rick was the next to storm out.

After contemplating for a second, I grabbed Orlando's plate along with mine and left the dining room, not wanting to see how things would go. I had to find Orlando.

"Where did he go?" I asked one of the staff, who pointed me toward the rooftop. "Thanks. Can you bring some milk and juice?"

"Sure, Miss."

When I reached the rooftop, Orlando was staring into the distance. The blue t-shirt he wore this morning stretched, emphasizing the muscles underneath as his hands tightened around the steel railing. I placed the plates on the table before going to him.

"Hey," I called softly, and when he didn't turn, I went to stand beside him, gazing at the sea.

"What are you doing here?" His voice was strained.

"Just coming to see if you were okay."

"I'm not okay."

"I can see that."

"I want to be alone," he said, not looking at me.

A part of me wanted to leave and give him the space he needed. But wasn't he alone all this time? He lived alone in an apartment close to his office and away from the Cortez mansion. He visited his family every weekend, but the only time he spent with them was during dinner.

How did I know all this? The answer was simple—Mike. He often spoke about his cousin and said how worried they were.

"I'm not leaving," I said in a determined voice. "You're either telling me what's going on in your mind or eating that breakfast with me."

Orlando whirled around with anger blazing in his eyes. "Don't push me, Ari."

A smile tugged at my lips. This was the first time he called me Ari. "I told you everything, Orlando. You were there to hold me when I needed someone. It's only fair that I wanted to be there for you."

"I don't need anyone."

I shrugged. "I'm not leaving."

"Then I'll leave." I caught his hand when he tried to walk away. "Ari—"

I stood on my toes and grabbed his head before pulling him down to kiss his lips. I didn't know why I did that, but I felt that was the only way to get his attention. Orlando was too shocked to move at first. His body went stiff, and his lips didn't move. *He did say he wouldn't reject me.*

I was beginning to regret my decision when I felt his hands grab my ass, and his mouth took control. Under a second, I was hoisted up. Helping me to hook my legs around his waist, he grabbed my hair and tipped my head, deepening the kiss.

Blood pounded in my veins as his hot tongue swept through my mouth, possessing me. My tongue lost its battle, and my eyes rolled back in my skull as his skillful lips sucked mine. His hands were all over my back, kneading my skin. I gasped when he gripped my ass, massaging the flesh. It sent shivers all over my body.

Every cell in my body came alive. I ran my hands over his chest, feeling the taut muscles under my palms. Orlando bit my lip when I gripped his hair, which was smooth and silky under my touch.

Our breathing grew harsher as wetness pooled between my thighs, a rare occurrence with Brian. My body stiffened at the thought of my ex, and Orlando stopped as if sensing the change in me.

"We can't do this," he said as he rested his forehead against mine. Our chests moved in a rhythm, matching our harsh breathing. This was the second time he was stopping it.

"Why not? We're adults."

"What if we can't be more?"

"I don't expect more." My reply was immediate. I was disappointed, but I was quick to mask it. "I like what we have now, and I don't want to ruin it."

"I'm not sure." His eyes closed. "I want you, Arianna, and it scares me." His hand cupped my cheek. "You wanted to know my story. My trust was betrayed by someone I loved. She said and did things that destroyed me, left me scarred. I don't know if I'll ever be someone you want." I waited as he took a deep breath. His thumb caressed my cheek. "You deserve someone better than me."

I shook my head. "I thought Brian was better, but look where it got me. Can't we just live in the moment?"

"I should have kept my distance from you, but when I saw your pain, I couldn't help reaching out. I feel like I'm taking advantage of this situation, Arianna."

"You're not," I whispered. "I'm a willing participant."

"You don't understand. I refuse to use you as a distraction."

A pang of guilt pierced my heart. Did he know I was doing the same thing? Wasn't I using him as a distraction? It wasn't completely true, though.

"Orlando..."

"I might be scarred, Arianna. But I know better than to use you just because you're willingly giving yourself to me. No, I won't do that to you. You are not someone I want to fuck."

"I understand." My reply was laced with hurt. I didn't know what to make of his words. He said he wanted me, and now he said he didn't want to fuck. I shouldn't have pushed him.

Orlando tipped my chin, forcing me to meet his gaze. "I won't have sex with you to blow off my anger. You're someone I want to make love with. There is a difference, Arianna," he explained.

A sudden rush of warmth filled my chest, slowly spreading to other parts of my body. "Then make love to me."

"Arianna--"

"I want you as much as you want me, Orlando. I know this is too early, but I've never been this sure before. I don't expect anything from you. I'll take what you offer."

"Ari--"

"No, let me speak. I'm tired of waiting on the sidelines for things to happen. I'm taking control of my life. I don't want to lose you, Orlando. We understand each other, and I know you won't hurt me."

"But what happens if someday I can't offer what you want?"

"No expectations, remember? Can we not talk about this and just live one day at a time? Let's just be Orlando and Arianna, who like each other's company."

"It's easier said than done."

I cupped his cheek. "Let's not make any rules. Forget we even had this conversation. Let's just do things that make us happier."

"Okay," Orlando reluctantly agreed. The smile on his face was all I wanted to see.

"I have something to take care of." He let me go and took my hands in his. His thumb circled in my palm.

"Okay. I'm sorry about the way she spoke to you."

It was nothing. Isabel didn't have my respect, and it didn't matter what she said or did. "I don't care." I threw my arms around him, wanting to feel him closer. My cheeks rested just above his heart, listening to the rhythm of its beat. "You had something to do." I pulled away after a while.

"Oh, yes." He cleared his throat. Nervous hands smoothed out the non-existent creases on his t-shirt. "I'll...um..."

"Don't ruin the moment." As cute as his nervousness looked, I was also scared he'd spoil it by saying something.

"Hmm...right."

My heart fluttered as if it was the first time I was meeting the man of my dreams. He was the first man who made my heart pound. In a way, I was glad things were finally working out in some way. With a smile that said, 'I'll see you later,' I left him to do whatever he wanted to do. I decided to give him space to work the things out for himself. In fact, I needed time too.

One step at a time, Ari, I told myself as I went looking for my friends.

***

I was surprised to see the pit bull sitting at my door, looking lost. I had just returned from the kitchen after grabbing a snack for the evening. Orlando had gone to the city after our conversation that morning. He was meeting their family lawyer.

"Boxer!"

The dog's ears perked up at the mention of his name. I was confused at first, wondering if it was Boxer since I had seen him only in pictures. Contrary to what others thought of a pit bull, Boxer was a shy dog. He was tortured and abused by his previous owner before being used for dog fights.

When I first heard Orlando adopted a dog, I was surprised. Orlando wasn't a dog person. None of the Cortezes was. They owned no pets. Now I looked at Boxer, I noticed the prominent scars on his body, partially hidden by his fur. His wide eyes held fear and pain, something that tugged at my heartstrings.

Now I understood why Orlando took him in. It took one broken soul to recognize another. I sat on the floor a few feet away from the dog. His head lowered, and his tail thumped the wooden door as droplets of pee leaked onto the floor.

"Hey, it's okay. I won't hurt you," I said in a calm voice. "Are you lost?" The dog licked its snout as a whine escaped from his mouth. "Aww...it's okay."

I wanted to reach out and touch him but wasn't sure how he'd react. I'd read somewhere to be careful around frightened animals. Feeling cornered with no means of escape usually forced them to attack or put severe stress on them. Changing my mind, I stood. I had to earn his trust first.

"Come, I'll take you to Orlando's room." Boxer's ears twitched when he heard Orlando's name, but he made no move to stand.

"Come on, aren't you a good boy? Let's go meet your papa." I turned around and took a few steps. "Boxer, don't you want to see Orlando?" A smile tugged at my lips when I noticed the pit bull following me nervously.

I continued to walk ahead with encouraging words to the dog. When I turned around the corner, the dog took off, his sudden movement surprising me. Loud cries erupted from within his chest as I now noticed Orlando hugging him.

"It's okay. I'm here now," Orlando said in a low voice as he rubbed Boxer's fur.

"Thanks for bringing him. I was looking for him everywhere," Orlando told me. "He knows how to open the door. He must've gotten out in search of me."

"I found him at my door. He is such a sweetheart."

"Boxer," Orlando cupped the dog's face, "meet Arianna. She's a friend."

Boxer gave me a bark and wagged his tail before burying his head in Orlando's shoulder.

"I've never left him for this long. When my stay got extended, I had him brought here on a yacht. He arrived an hour ago," Orlando explained. "He never met so many people before."

"Don't worry. Take it slow. When he sees we're harmless, he'll relax."

I jumped when I felt something wet in my hand. When I looked down, Boxer was sniffing at me as he circled me with a newfound interest. I chuckled softly as I waited for him to imprint on my scent.

"He likes you."

"I like him too. Can I touch you, boy?" Boxer sat down beside me before putting his paw on my extended hand to shake. I laughed and placed a kiss on his head. "I'll leave you both to settle down. See you at dinner."

"Sure."

Chapter 14

Nine days had passed, and three days since our conversation. A lot had happened, and I was happier than I'd been in a long time. I never knew just a few days was enough to take my mind off certain things. But in truth, I was never over the crush on Orlando. It felt right in every sense. Sometimes, I thanked my fate for bringing Brian into my life. If it wasn't for the heartbreak, Orlando wouldn't have felt the need to get closer.

Isabel was removed from the property, and everyone was back to normal after that. The wedding date drew closer. While Brian poked his head in my mind once in a while, all I felt now was shame and anger at myself. I was furious for not seeing through his facade. Shameful for trusting him and for allowing him to jerk me around.

I had no way of knowing. Even moving in again with my parents was temporary. I was going to move out as soon as I found a job, which I already had with Orlando's recommendation.

A smile broke past my lips at the thought. This morning, he surprised me with my interview at one of his firms and even arranged for a place for me to stay nearby. It was a decent studio apartment overlooking the city of Linnesse, and I was excited.

However, my happiness didn't last because he informed me that he was traveling to Europe after the wedding. Mike's words surfaced in my mind as I masked my hurt and wished him luck for the important negotiations he told us about.

If Orlando caught my distress, he didn't show it. He expressed his worries about leaving Boxer for so long. When he asked if I could check on Boxer once in a while, I readily agreed. I realized he wanted me to be a part of his life, even if it extended only to caring for his dog. *Will he miss me? Does he feel the same way about me?*

Orlando was looking forward to this trip. That much was clear. This was planned almost six months ago, and though I wished he'd change his mind, I knew it wouldn't be possible. I couldn't be selfish when I knew this trip would bring in more business opportunities. Thousands of families depended on Cortez businesses, and Orlando's success meant they all had jobs.

A deep sigh left my lips as I caressed Boxer's fur. We lounged on the balcony, which gave me a wonderful view of the sea. My phone beeped with a notification, and I opened my Instagram to see new comments on my recent post.

Alana's friends had stopped posting mean comments, and suddenly, they all went silent. Her Instagram was now full of images that were related to the wedding. Every morning and night, she posted a selfie of her and Brian with a love quote, saying how blessed she was to have him in her life.

Brian's smile was effortless, and he wasn't looking over his shoulder, worrying if anyone would see them. Looking at the photo again, I now remember the constant concern on his face whenever we met in public places. He'd stopped taking me to restaurants after two months and instead cooked dinner in his apartment. At the time, I thought he was being romantic. It was only now I realized he was being careful.

What was going on in his mind when he courted me? Did Alana know about this? Of course, she did. I mean, she saw us together several times and never seemed to care. My head began to ache, and I massaged my temples. What was their sick game? Was I some kind of bet? Did Alana want me broken so badly that she had her boyfriend seduce me?

Whatever it was, I was glad it was over. While it hurt more than it should, I looked at the positive side of things. Orlando wasn't open with his feelings, and to be honest, I wasn't either. I needed a distraction, and Orlando was conveniently near.

But was that all he was to me? Definitely not. A painful breath stretched my lungs, and I felt an ache in my heart. I knew Orlando was more, but I was afraid to admit it and even more fearful to express it to him. What if he didn't want more?

I should stick to my original plan. No expectations. The thing with Orlando was I couldn't risk it. If things escalated and didn't work out the way I wanted, I would lose him forever. He wouldn't be there even as a friend. I wasn't ready to lose him, never. That much I knew. I wanted Orlando to be a part of my life, if not as a lover, then at least as a friend.

My poor brain failed to comprehend how hard it was to return once that fine line was crossed. *You both have crossed it several times already,* my conscience pointed out. We did. Though we didn't kiss again, we often cozied up to each other at night, talking. We often woke up next morning in each other's arms. It felt more intimate than the kiss we shared.

"What's happening to me?" I groaned, wanting to pull my hair. *Why am I thinking of all this now?* I was supposed to enjoy this evening as my friends enjoyed their time in town. They'd gone to a local club to grab a few drinks and dance their asses off. I feigned a headache and stayed back, wanting to enjoy the solitude. What was happening now was the exact opposite of what I had in mind.

I should've gone with them.

I got up and walked to my room, wondering where Orlando was. I hadn't seen him all day. Boxer showed up in my room just after lunch, and we'd been hanging out since then.

"Hey, boy, did your papa tell where he was going?" I asked Boxer as I went down to the kitchen. I was bored, and when I was bored, I always craved junk food.

The kitchen buzzed with activities for dinner, and the staff greeted me with warm smiles before going back to whatever they were doing. I went to the refrigerator and was delighted to find the leftover cake from last night's dessert.

I served myself a generous amount before grabbing an ice cream tub and a few bags of chips. My cheeks stretched with a smile as I had everything I wanted. Today, I was treating myself. There was a bounce in my step when I exited the kitchen.

Once again, I couldn't help but compare the sense of freedom I had in Orlando and Mike's home. If I paraded in my tank top and tight shorts at my home, there would be several sets of judgemental eyes drilling holes in my skull. They just never realized there were more important things in this world than Gucci or Prada. What was the point of dolling yourself with expensive brands when your soul smelled worse than a pile of horse shit?

What else can I do? Maybe a movie marathon, or maybe I could just listen to music and paint my nails. Boxer was eyeing the goodies when I set them on the table. I almost felt guilty for not grabbing his dog treats. But again, I could always share my treats with him.

I winked at him as I took the first bite of the cake. I had forgotten the name of the Indian dessert that was full of rich cream, almonds, and pistachios. It tasted like heaven, and my taste buds longed for more. Boxer tilted his head as I indulged with greedy spoonsful.

"Do you want some?" I asked, and he responded with a bark, his tail thumping on the floor. "Go ahead and bring your plate, then. We'll share."

Boxer dashed out of the room like a bat out of hell, and before I knew it, he was back with his plate safely clutched in his mouth. He dropped it gently beside my leg and drooled with his eyes fixated on my dessert bowl, which was almost empty. He was well-trained and well-behaved. He surprised me often. With a grunt, I gave the rest to him and picked up the packet of chips.

***

Jessie J and Nicki Minaj sang at the top of their lungs. A giggle tumbled past my lips as I twerked in front of the mirror. It started with me singing out loud and Boxer's howl as I painted my nails. After a while, he started chasing his tail and jumping when the music changed, which made me join him.

I'd never seen a dog dancing before. He shook his butt and wagged his tail. I saw the real happiness on Boxer's face as we ran around the room, chasing each other. Boxer loved music. He seemed to like my choice of songs.

We were dancing for a while, and when I twirled, I noticed someone in my peripheral vision, and my footing slipped. Orlando was there, catching me before I fell on my butt. *When did he get here?*

I regained my composure and steadied myself. Looking around, I realized Boxer was nowhere around. *Bugger! Couldn't he at least give me a warning before bailing on me?*

"That was a wonderful performance, Arianna."

The booming music had nothing to do with the butterflies that fluttered in my belly. His pupils were dilated, and his gaze didn't mask the desire as it swept over me. I felt his heated gaze caressing me like a feather.

"I liked watching you dance."

My breath hitched, and I averted my gaze, unable to hold his anymore.

Orlando hooked his finger under my chin. "Will you dance for me?"

"Ah... I..."

"Please..."

I bit my lower lip, contemplating it for a moment. Brian never asked me to dance for him. I remember how offended he looked when he saw me dance with Rosie when we went clubbing together. He'd said he saw no difference between me and a hooker.

"Okay," I agreed, shoving aside thoughts of Brian. Orlando respected me, and there was no mockery in his eyes. They held pure admiration, and I couldn't lie about the sudden urge to show him my moves.

Orlando changed the music, and I felt a deep blush creep onto my cheeks when the song began to play. Ciara's voice sent chills down my body. *Did he know I had this song?* It fit the mood perfectly. He moved to close the curtains.

When he returned, I couldn't take my eyes off him. Orlando's eyes never left mine as he shrugged off his leather jacket. The thin V-neck t-shirt emphasized his taut muscles. I could only gasp as he pulled me to him, both his hands on my waist. His forehead rested on mine as he began to move, a slow and sensual motion that set my veins on fire.

I found my body moving in rhythm with him. Orlando twirled me around before pressing my back to his chest. I threw my head back when he rolled his hips against me. When his nose ran along the skin on my neck, my flesh erupted with goosebumps. His hands traced the length of my body as he moved me around. When he dipped me, I wanted his lips on mine. Orlando, however, was on a mission.

He knew what he was doing. He'd let me feel the heat of his body before moving away and twirling me around. His lips would grace my skin, leaving me breathless. His hands would cup the swell of my breasts, tracing the outline but never touching the way I wanted. He would squeeze my ass before stroking his hands on my inner thighs.

I ran my hands along his strong chest, rolling his t-shirt up and feeling the warm skin against my palms. The growing bulge in his pants brushed against my hip, pressing into me once in a while. My hips rotated, grinding against his hardness as he turned me again.

Our combined breathing and the growing heat clouded my mind as wetness pooled down south. By the time the song ended, I was lying on my back on the soft mattress as his body hovered over mine. I moaned even before his lips touched mine, my body overly sensitive to his every touch. The feeling overwhelmed my senses.

I trembled with anticipation as he finally relented. I writhed under his hands, arching my back while begging him with my moans.

Chapter 15

I lay breathless, my eyes rolled back into my skull as his lips took possession of my mouth again. His fingers were still buried deep in me. Orlando's thumb applied pressure on my bundle of nerves, making my body jerk. Climbing down from the high, every inch of my apex was still sensitive to his touch.

When his lips finally released mine, I opened my eyes to peer into his lust-filled gray ones. That was my best and first orgasm at the hands of a man. A gasp left my mouth when he pulled his fingers out. I looked between us to see my virgin blood coating them, and I felt a blush creep onto my cheeks.

"I'm sorry about that," I muttered, mild embarrassment lacing my voice.

Orlando's smile was unfazed. "This isn't something I'd be embarrassed about," he whispered thickly. "This is an honor. Thanks for giving it to me, Arianna."

His words dumbfounded me, and I felt those weird feelings snaking into my heart, taking possession. *What is he doing to me?* "You're welcome, I guess."

Orlando pecked my lips before getting up. "I'll be right back."

I adjusted my clothes as I tried to catch my breath. One second, we were dancing, and the next, I was writhing under him with pleasure. There was a mild ache in my sweet spot. It was mourning the loss of his fingers. My heart fluttered while thinking how intimate we had become. I still couldn't comprehend why he wouldn't go all the way when he had my consent.

"As much as I'd like to stay, I have to leave now," Orlando said when he came in. "I have a conference call with one of our European clients in less than ten minutes." He checked his watch. "I'll see you at dinner tonight."

"Sure."

He turned to leave but seemed to have a change of heart before he came toward me, kissing me again.

***

The smell of barbeque roused my hunger as I lounged on a chair, watching my friends swim. The wedding was only two days away and we'd get busy with the festivities from tomorrow. My days here on the estate had been filled with activities, and for the first time in my life, I had a great vacation.

The girls were excited about everything and anything. Boxer had warmed up to everyone a bit, but he was most comfortable with me and Orlando, and he cozied up to me in the absence of his papa. Thoughts about Orlando consumed my being day and night. While I was feeling sad about his business trip, something in me looked forward to his return.

My phone beeped, distracting me from my thoughts. I had a few notifications and a message on my Instagram since I last checked.

Brian: We need to talk.

There was nothing to talk about.

Brian: I know you've seen my message. Stop ignoring me.

He was getting on my nerves. Did he think he had the right to talk to me after everything he had done?

Arianna: Oh, hello there, brother-in-law. Wassup?

Self-satisfaction filled me when I hit send. I could already imagine his handsome face growing red with anger.

Brian: I saw your photo on Instagram. The brunette look suits you well.

My heart flipped. No, it wasn't because of the feelings I had for him. Maybe a little. But, I recognized the majority of my emotions were fueled by anger and resentment. *Who does he think he is?*

Brian: It didn't take you long to find another guy.

If his previous message wasn't enough, this did it.

Arianna: It's funny, considering who's saying this. At least I cut ties with my ex before jumping into bed with another one.

Brian: Don't act smart.

Arianna: What do you want, Brian? There is nothing for us to talk about.

Brian: There is.

Brian: Look, I don't know why you're doing this. But this should stop.

I looked around me and then at the fresh smoothie in my hand. What was wrong with what I was doing now?

Arianna: What I do is not your concern, brother-in-law.

Brian: It's every bit my concern when what you do ruins my family's reputation. You're headed down a path of self-destruction.

Brian: You are ruining your life.

Arianna: You're wrong. I'm just living my life the way I want. I'll tell you one last time, Brian. Don't poke your nose in my business.

Brian: I won't if you keep your private matters private. I don't want to see any more photos of yours.

Arianna: Who do you think you are? Get the fuck out of my account and block me for all I care. I don't give a damn about your reputation. We are fucking over, and don't talk to me again.

I locked the phone and threw it on the table as I tried to calm my raging nerves. That bastard. What was he thinking? I shouldn't have replied to him.

Fuck!

He ruined my mood.

"What's bothering you?" A pair of strong hands massaged my bare shoulders, and I relaxed instantly.

"See for yourself." I waved toward my phone.

Orlando picked it up with a puzzled look before swiping his thumb across the screen. The phone lit up, showing the screen saver, which was a photo of Orlando pecking my cheek at the costume party. His lips stretched as he cast me a questioning look.

"Check my Instagram inbox," I answered while trying to hide the fluttering of my heart. I wasn't thinking when I told him to check my phone. I wondered what was on his mind as he read the messages.

"What does he want?" Orlando's voice took a hard edge as he returned the phone. His eyes were narrowed and flashing with anger.

"I'm not sure." I sighed. "But I have an idea about what I want to do."

Orlando raised his eyebrow in question before I climbed on his lap, pulling him closer. A knowing smile spread on his lips. "Let them burn," I whispered, closing the distance between our lips.

My initial plan was to take a selfie of us kissing, but the thoughts flew out of my mind when our lips touched. The phone was long forgotten as his tongue laced with mine.

Brian and my family can all go to hell.

***

"That was one hell of a show you put on for us." Rosie winked.

Chiara handed us both our drinks before taking a seat beside us. It was one of the rare moments we had for ourselves. I loved it here. We were mostly spending our time at the beach. Now, we lay on the sand as we admired the orange hues of the sky. The guys were playing soccer a few yards away.

"Yeah," Skyler agreed.

"You complain as if you were being modest with Jeff. You guys are always at it like rabbits."

Skyler snickered. "And our influence is rubbing on you too."

"A little." I grinned, shaking my head.

"So, how was it?" Rosie asked, and her eyes filled with amusement.

I looked at the guys. Orlando effortlessly kicked the ball, chasing it to the goal. He laughed when Enrique tackled him. It was something we didn't see often. "It was good. We didn't go all the way, though."

"What? She's kidding, right?" Chiara asked.

"Shush, girl. They might hear us." Rosie silenced her.

Sitting up, I grabbed a drink. "No. We danced, and we made out."

"And?" Skyler asked, grabbing a drink for herself.

"Um...he touched me...there." My cheeks heated up.

"So, you're telling us that you guys got intimate, but there was no penetration."

I pinched my best friend a bit harder. "That sounded ugly."

"I was just stating the fact," Rosie said defensively. "I mean, that's the meaning of 'we touched, but we didn't go all the way,' isn't it?"

"Yeah," Skyler and Chiara agreed.

"Give her some credit, Rosie. They got somewhere, didn't they?" Skyler sided with me.

"Of course," Rosie said. "But it isn't enough. Tell us what's stopping you. Don't tell us there are cockblockers here."

"I don't know. He wouldn't do it, even after I told him I wanted to."

"Hmm..." Rosie looked thoughtful. "Do you know anything about his ex?"

I shook my head. "He won't talk about his past."

"Let them take it slow," Chiara piped in. "We're surprised that Orlando has come out of his shell for once. We want this to last. Uncle Rick and Grandpapa approve of you, Arianna. They know you're good for Orlando."

"I'm not going to expect anything at this point. We both have been betrayed. I don't want to jump to conclusions."

"It's okay, Ari." Rosie patted my thigh. "Take it slow and keep an open mind. Just know that you'll always have us with you, no matter what happens, okay?"

"Okay."

"Show me Brian's message," Rosie demanded suddenly. I handed her my phone and waited as she read the message. "Did Orlando say anything?"

"No."

She appeared thoughtful for a moment. "Why would he spew the same bullshit as your family? You're with your friends. What did he mean by the path of self-destruction?"

Chiara took my phone from her hand, and Skyler poked her head in, reading our conversation.

"Something is fishy," Skyler agreed.

"Be careful around him, Ari. I think your sister has something to do with it," Rosie said.

I shrugged. "I don't care anymore. It's not my problem." Not anymore. I meant every word. While his betrayal still stung, I taught myself not to dwell on it anymore. The pain motivated me to live a better life before the people who wanted to see me perish. If life taught me one thing, it was not to cry over spilled milk. In Brian's case, he was not just spilled milk, he was spoiled. He didn't deserve my tears.

Rosie told me once that the pain of the betrayal would always be there. We could only learn to forget and move on. I wanted to go as far as possible from Alana and Brian. However, I'd attend this wedding not because I wanted to see them exchange vows and rings. I agreed to go not because I wanted to bless the happy couple. I would go because I didn't want them to think I was a coward. It would change nothing, but it would give me satisfaction.

I decided to check my Instagram since it'd been a while. There were a lot of posts from Rosie. Laughter bubbled in my throat when I stumbled on photos of the hot men we met at the beach today. It turned out that Orlando hadn't hired just one lifeguard. He had a team of them stationed across the private beach.

I noticed Enrique was reckless as always, and despite several warnings, he got in the water after drinking. It worried me that he couldn't care less about his life, and it also warmed my heart knowing how Orlando cared for his brother. Rosie had posted so many photos of the lifeguards. *Jeff's hands are full with this one.* I shook my head with a smile.

"Enrique should be careful with his drinking habits." Rosie turned to Chiara. "The lifeguards can't always be with him, you know," she said, voicing my thoughts.

Chiara smiled. "I know. It worries me a lot, but he promised he wouldn't touch alcohol after our wedding."

"That sounds good." Skyler patted her hand.

"Enrique hasn't looked at another woman since you came into his life. I'm sure he'll change for the better," I told her. Enrique used to be a playboy, the exact opposite of Orlando. He dated models and actresses. No one thought he would settle down this early. Chiara changed him for good.

Chiara smiled. "Thanks, Ari."

"Holy smokes! Look at them," Rosie gushed, distracting us, and I turned to see the lifeguards parading on the sand with only their swim trunks that hung low on their hips.

"Your man is over there, Rosie." I pinched her arm.

"Stop that, bish! I was just looking."

"No more looking for you now."

Rosie rolled her eyes. "My eyes won't be starved, and looking is allowed."

"Preach, girl." Our laughter rhymed with the ocean waves, my heart feeling lighter than when I first arrived.

Chapter 16

B rian Schultz

"Brian...that's too much carb. You have to be fit for our wedding."

My jaw clenched as I glared at Alana before pulling the bowl closer. "Stop telling me what to eat," I hissed under my breath as she looked around the table, smiling sweetly.

"Others are listening."

"Then you should just shut your mouth and concentrate on your food." There was only so much a man could take. For the third time today, she made me question my decision to marry her. Maybe I should've waited. But it wasn't like I had a choice.

Alana turned her attention to her friends, chatting while I shoveled my favorite chicken casserole into my mouth. It had been a week since I'd had proper food. She tried to control every aspect of my life, which I didn't appreciate.

"Here is your dessert, sir." The waiter placed the delicious chocolate mousse in front of me.

"I think you brought the wrong order. We ordered fruit salad."

"That's my order." I cut her off.

Her face changed, not that I gave a damn about it. I didn't have to be told what I could or couldn't eat. I had kept myself fit for twenty-six years before she came into my life.

Alana stayed quiet until the dinner was over, and when it was time to leave, everyone posed for a selfie while I excused myself to the bathroom. I took a deep breath and tried to control my growing anger. I didn't know why I was getting agitated. Maybe it was because of Arianna. I pinched the bridge of my nose, trying to suppress my irritation.

When I exited and walked to my car, I knew what questions I would face.

"You talked to her again, didn't you?" Alana's voice was innocent, her face crestfallen. I almost felt bad for telling her off.

"No."

"My friends noticed what happened. You embarrassed me in front of them, Brian. Why would you do that?"

"Maybe the next time, you should stop trying to make decisions for me," I snapped. "We're getting married, but it doesn't mean you have to try to control everything about my life."

"Is that what you think of me?" Her voice cracked. "I was just looking out for you."

"Don't."

I cursed when her sobs grew louder. Fuck! I hated it when she did this. My grip tightened around the steering wheel as I stepped on the gas. My brain conjured several words I wanted to yell at her, and I had to bite the inside of my cheeks to stop them.

Not now.

When we reached our home, she ran inside. I sat in the car for a moment longer, wondering what went wrong. My thoughts were once again consumed by Arianna. I still remember the day I stumbled onto her.

It was my parents' decision that I marry the Swansons' daughter, their business partners, and friends. I never said no to my parents' demands, and when I met Alana during a conference in New York, she was everything I wanted. A perfect wife and a daughter-in-law. She was a beauty to behold, and I had asked her out right away.

Our parents were elated and were already planning for our marriage. A month later, I was meeting Alana and her friends in a restaurant when I stumbled upon her in the parking lot. I had never seen Alana dressed down before, and it was startling seeing her in jean shorts and a tank top. A leather jacket hung loosely in her arms. Her untamed hair and wild eyes caught me off guard. I was so used to her formal socialite attire that this look surprised me.

"Oh, I'm sorry." She tried to smile, but her eyes said otherwise.

Before I could ask what was wrong, my phone rang. I frowned when I saw it, and when I looked up, she was gone.

"Hey, Brian," Alana's chirpy voice greeted me as my gaze swept the parking lot. Was this a prank?

"Hey, I'm here."

"Great! My friends are so excited to see you. Come on in."

When I went in, Alana was at her best, wearing a tailored knee-length Gucci dress. The image of the girl from the parking lot flashed in my mind as I took a seat beside her.

Now, I reclined in my seat, watching the light going on in our bedroom. I didn't want to go in right away. Her tears tired me.

Arianna rarely cried. She was strong and bold. She was everything Alana would never be. A deep sigh left my lips as my thoughts raced.

I was intrigued by the girl I met in the parking lot, and I soon learned who she was. The truth stunned me. She was Alana's twin.

Their differences surprised me. While Alana was polished, Arianna was rough around the edges.

I found myself thinking more about her, and whenever I was with Alana, I couldn't help but wonder what it would be like to be with Arianna. I wasn't thinking clearly when I asked her out, something I regretted until now. I should've stayed true to Alana, but I couldn't.

I had to know. By then, Arianna ruled my thoughts. The more I learned about her, the more I wanted to be with her. I loved her free-spirited nature. She spoke her mind and was brutally honest. With her, my life was never boring.

While Alana seemed like a well-trained wife material, Arianna was a breath of fresh air and gave me an adrenaline rush every time we were together. Three months had passed, and I was head over heels for Arianna. It was only a matter of getting our parents' blessing.

The light in our bedroom went off, and I stepped out of the car, taking a deep breath. We lived alone, and though I owned this place, I felt like a foreigner here. No, it didn't feel like home. It wasn't my choice. I never wanted to stay in the heart of the city.

When my legs moved on autopilot to the entrance, I took in the landscape and the decorations. It made me realize how much had changed over the months. Alana never consulted me when she purchased this home or when she chose the interiors. It was all her choice.

Instead of going to the bedroom, I walked to the bar, pouring myself a generous glass of whiskey. I needed it now more than ever. My nerves were a wreck. When the amber liquid touched my lips, I welcomed the familiar burn. I could feel the drink traveling past my sternum as it filled my mouth with a bitter taste.

Why?

Why hadn't things worked out for me?

For us?

When Arianna told me that my mother never liked her, I didn't take it seriously. I thought she had misunderstood. But when I saw my mother's hatred toward Arianna at one of the parties, I knew my chances of getting their blessing were slim.

As for Alana, she laughed in my face when I said I loved her sister. "You're a fool, Brian. What does she have that I can't give you?"

"Everything," I answered.

Alana shook her head with a knowing smirk. "It won't work. Your mom hates her."

"I'll take care of that."

Alana shrugged, but I could tell that she was furious. "I'm not telling my parents anything now. Do whatever you want. When you realize she isn't the one for you, I'll be here." She had walked away without looking back.

With Alana out of the way, now it was my parents. I needed them to accept Arianna because my father hadn't given me a permanent position in his company yet. I also knew he wouldn't hesitate to throw me out if I ever vocalized my feelings for the rebellious twin. At times, I worried Alana would ruin my plans by telling them, but she kept her mouth shut.

When I found no way to tell them, I resorted to the only thing I knew. I began to change Arianna to fit in. It was the only way I could make them see the difference. I had to prove to them that she could change. I believed if they saw her new personality, they would agree.

It almost happened when they sent Alana and me on a business trip to Europe. I decided to talk to my parents after my return. Arianna cried when she said goodbye.

However, once in Europe, things went south. I ended up in bed with Alana after having a few drinks, and it became a habit. I missed Arianna, and her look-alike was there in flesh and blood. It wasn't like we'd never had sex before, but we stopped being together when things became serious with Arianna.

I knew what I was doing was wrong in every sense. I shouldn't be sleeping with both sisters. Though I planned to break up with Alana several times, I couldn't. Every night, she'd come to my room, and I ended up fucking her. The fact that they were identical didn't help me in the least. To me, it was Arianna.

I often fantasized about Arianna as I fucked her sister. When I looked down at her face, it was Arianna I saw, and it was perfect. When I woke up in the morning beside her, I'd tell myself that I'd tell her the truth. But the thin line between right and wrong vanished as I found myself giving in day after day.

When it was time for us to return, I spoke to Alana again. "We should stop this. I can't do this to her."

Alana looked down as tears gathered in her eyes. "Have you ever thought about my feelings, Brian? I love you too. Why her? Why it isn't me?"

"I'm sorry, Alana. You know why. She's different."

"You didn't think that when we slept together," her pained voice hissed. "Look at me, Brian. We have the same face, eyes, hair, even voice. What's so wrong with me that you want her and not me?"

"Alana..."

"It's okay. I get it, Brian. But tell me this. What are you going to do about our baby?"

"Baby?"

Alana nodded. "I just found out. What do you think Arianna will do when she finds out? She'll know you were sleeping with me behind her back."

"She'll never know the truth. We have to do something."

"I'm keeping the baby, Brian."

"Alana—"

"I'm sorry, Brian. I knew you would plan something like this." She wiped her tears. "I've already informed your mother. They're meeting us at the airport when we land."

"*What?*"

"You have no choice but to marry me, Brian. My sister will never want you when she learns the truth. The best thing would be for you to keep your mouth shut and pretend like it never happened." Her voice had taken a sharp edge as her features hardened. It almost felt like she planned all this. But then, I should've known better. There was no excuse for what I did.

A humorless chuckle left my lips as I chugged the rest of the liquid down my throat. I couldn't wipe off the look of horror and pain on Arianna's face. I saw her storm out of the ballroom. I saw her tears, yet I was a selfish fool.

"Aren't you coming to bed?"

I turned and saw Alana, who was dressed in a silk nightie. Her tummy was still flat, making me wonder if she was really pregnant, but I had seen the sonogram and concluded she wouldn't have lied to me.

While I didn't want to go to bed yet, I reminded myself that she was the mother of my unborn child. I knew better than to cause any distress. "You should be resting." My voice was softer than before.

"I couldn't sleep."

"Come, I'll lie down with you." I stood and walked toward our bedroom.

"Do you still love her?" Alana asked when we lay in the darkness of the room.

"No."

"I want this to work more than anything, Brian. I love you. I can't imagine a life without you."

I couldn't respond. I didn't want to tell her the same.

"What will make you love me more, Brian?"

Nothing. I wanted to tell her, but I held my tongue. It was my mistake from the beginning. I was too sheltered by my parents, and I didn't get to experience the world outside the elite circle they drew for me. I was trained how to laugh and speak in public. They'd trained me to mask my emotions.

Meeting Ariana had changed me forever. For the first time, she showed me things I never knew existed. I felt free when I was with her.

"I asked you a question, Brian."

Once again, I couldn't help but wonder how Arianna would've reacted in a situation like this. Her face would grow redder as she yelled at me. She knew how to push my buttons. Arianna would show real emotions. I knew Alana wanted to cry out and shake me by my collar. Was it necessary to hide her emotions when we were alone? Why did she have to put her mask on, even in our private space?

"Be real, Alana. I want you to be real."

"But—"

"I'm tired. Let's go to sleep, please."

Alana didn't speak another word, and I relaxed. Inhaling, her perfume clouded my senses. I held her tighter, once again imagining her as Arianna.

Chapter 17

The Cortez estate glowed like it was Christmas again. The exterior expanse of the mansion and garden was decorated with lights. Bouquets made of natural flowers decorated every corridor. Unlike the exterior, the decorations inside were minimal. However, the grand interior design compensated for the lack of other items, and the fragrance of the flowers made the environment pleasant.

Boxer stayed by my side as I ambled my way through the staff, buzzing with activities. Orlando asked if I could dog-sit for a night, and I agreed. The men were at the guest house celebrating Enrique's last night as a bachelor. They whisked Enrique away, claiming he shouldn't see the bride until tomorrow.

"Arianna, did you see my daughter?" Chiara's mom inquired when we bumped into each other.

"She's with the girls."

"Oh, she's not answering her phone. I'm heading out with her dad. His brother and family are arriving tonight. Please look after her for me, will you? She's so nervous." Her face was full of concern for her daughter, and it made me wish my mom was like that.

"Skyler snatched her phone when she wouldn't stop checking it. Don't worry, Chiara is our responsibility."

"Thank you so much, sweetie. I knew I could rely on you. By the way, how do I look?" She patted her hair, which was held up in a neat bun, giving her an elegant yet formal look. She wore a knee-length dress with a high neckline that snuggled against her lithe figure.

"You look perfect as always, Camilla."

She let out a relieved breath before hugging me. "Thank God. Did I tell you my mother-in-law is also coming with them?" she whispered. "I swear the old goat never liked me. She always found reasons to degrade me in front of the rest of the family."

"You are gorgeous, Camilla. If she can't see that, perhaps she should get her eyes checked." Chiara's mom still looked young, with olive skin similar to Chiara's. There was always a smile on her face, which added a crown to her naturally beautiful look. Her insecurity surprised me. I wondered why her family didn't come earlier. Now it appeared they didn't have a good relationship.

Camilla beamed. "You are such a sweetheart. I'm glad Chi has friends like you with her." She checked her watch. "I have to go. Chi's father isn't a patient man, especially when his family is involved."

"Sure. I'll see you tomorrow."

Camilla hurried outside, and I ventured back toward my room. Chiara said she didn't want a bachelorette party and she'd rather spend her time with us. While they could've gone somewhere else for their honeymoon, Chiara preferred to spend it here, so there wasn't much for us to do.

Suddenly, I was pulled into a room and pinned against a wall. "Orlando!" It had become a habit of his. While I hated being surprised, I thought it was romantic. Though Orlando said he wasn't ready to offer me more, his actions proved otherwise. My logical side reminded me that I could be misreading the signs, but who could blame me? Wouldn't any girl react this way when her crush finally paid attention to her? I could only hope this worked for us.

His chuckle warmed my insides, and his hands caressed my length. "You shouldn't be here." This would lead to my own doom, I knew, but I couldn't control my galloping heart. *No expectations.* The warning went out the window when that mischievous look covered his face again.

"It's not like I'm the one getting married." He shrugged.

"You should be with Enrique."

"He's nervous."

We were distracted by a sudden commotion outside. "What's that?"

"Don't know." Orlando frowned, and we rushed out.

The security guards were removing the servants from the living area, and I tensed, seeing Enrique on his knees before Chiara, who was on the verge of tears. *What's going on?*

"Trust me, please. This isn't true."

"Did you meet her?"

"I did," Enrique said and quickly added, "Babe, it's not what you think."

"What do I think, Enrique?"

"Please let me explain. Nothing happened that day. I never touched another woman; please trust—"

Chiara raised her hand, stopping him in mid-sentence. "It's you who don't trust me, Enrique."

"What? No. No, I—"

She stopped him again. "If you trusted my love for you, you wouldn't be here begging for me to trust you."

"Babe..."

"I know these photos are perfectly timed to make you look guilty."

Rosie handed us the photographs in question, and we looked at them. *Whoa!* Enrique appeared to be kissing another woman, and in one photo, it appeared as if he was molesting her, while in truth, he was pushing her away. I vaguely remember Mike telling us about an incident involving a crazy stalker ex. *Is that her?*

Enrique sobbed with relief and pulled her into his embrace. "I'm sorry. She showed up in the office with her friend and demanded I give her two minutes."

"You didn't tell me."

"I didn't think it was important at the time. She said she's moving to Washington to be close to her parents. Then she moved to kiss my cheek, and then...then they left."

Chiara nodded, and the tension in the room diffused a little. "Never, ever hide something like this from me again."

"I won't."

Orlando clutched my hand, and I squeezed it reassuringly. When his gaze met mine, it conveyed things words couldn't explain. I was glad Enrique and Chiara sorted it out quickly. The trust she had for him was heart-warming.

"All right, enough for the night, ladies and gentlemen. It's time to get the bride and groom to their separate rooms." Jeff clapped his hands. "Enrique, buddy, if you had to see her, all you had to do is say so, or maybe you could've sneaked in. There's no need for all this."

I chuckled. Jeff had a way with his words, and he was the worst joker ever.

"I'll see you tomorrow," Orlando whispered in my ear before dragging Enrique away.

"I admire your love for each other," I said to Chiara while hugging her.

"Thank you."

"And wanna tell me what you were doing with Orlando?" Rosie nudged my ribs.

"Not now." I hushed her, making everyone laugh. "Let's get the bride to bed. We have a lot to do tomorrow."

***

Brian Schultz

"What's this?" I was taken aback by Alana's new look. For a moment, I thought it was *her*.

"I changed my hair color," Alana said. "I want you to love me the way you love her." She sniffled. "I don't care, even if I have to change who I am. I'll do anything for you, Brian."

Anger flared in my veins. They always looked alike and even used the same brand perfume. You couldn't tell them apart. However, when Arianna posted the photo on Instagram, it was clear she was moving on. She changed her look. Why would Alana want to look like her?

I shook my head. "I can't believe this." At least with her old style, I pretended she was Arianna. "I don't like this look on you."

"But I saw you staring at her photo. Isn't this what you wanted? I don't get it, Brian. Before you left for our business trip, all you did was try to change her to be like me. You almost succeeded in it. What's the issue now? You still get us both. I have the perfect qualities to be your socialite wife, and now I have her looks. What more do you need?"

I covered my face with my hands, counting back from ten. It was sick. But she also made me realize what I was doing with Arianna. Instead of accepting her for who she was, I tried to change her into someone else. Though I despised what Alana said, I couldn't deny the truth.

"Don't do anything like this again," I warned. "It makes me sick to my stomach."

"Brian!"

I turned to look at her. This was one of the rare times she showed her real emotions.

"Why am I not enough?"

"You know the answer perfectly well, Alana. Go ahead and change everything that's you. Get painted from head to toe. But that won't change you into her. She's the real deal. You...will never be her."

And my own words made me realize one thing. Arianna wouldn't have stayed the same either. It wasn't who she was. What a fool I was.

"I agree. I'll never be what she was," Alana hissed behind me. "I'll never party hard or fuck every guy I see."

Her words caught me off guard. I had to clench my jaw to stay quiet. I had seen her party pictures. *Isn't that why I tried to talk her out of it?*

"You see, Brian, she'll never be me. You were a fool to even think she'd be your perfect wife. She'll never give up her partying ways. You'd have always been her third wheel. She was using you to hurt me, Brian. How can you not see that? She never loved you!"

Without another word, I slammed the door behind me and left. My conversation with Arianna over Instagram surfaced in my memory. Her mocking words hit me harder this time. She'd said she was living her life. She kept addressing me as a brother-in-law, rubbing it in my face.

When we returned from our business trip, I wanted to apologize to Arianna and break up with her. But then, I saw the photos and was furious with her for leading a double life. I knew Arianna liked to party. I'd seen her twerk in the club with her friends. We even had a fight over her behavior. I thought she stopped going to clubs after that.

Fuck!

I hit the steering wheel. I'd been sitting in this car for a while now. I had pulled the car in one of the empty parking lots since I couldn't concentrate on the road anymore. *Why does my life have to be so complicated?* Then, another thing surprised me. Arianna and I never got intimate. She'd always stop me if I got bolder while kissing her. She never allowed me to touch her in an inappropriate manner.

But I recognized one of the photos where she was showing her ass to the camera, barely clad in a thong. If that wasn't enough, now, while the family prepared for the wedding, she was out there partying with the Cortez men. How did she know the Cortez men? My anger turned toward her friend Rosalinda. She must've introduced them. *Yeah, that must be it.*

The photos on their Instagram account went up shortly after their trip began, and I'd been following them religiously. Arianna appeared smiling in all the photos, and one photo—the one with Enrique Cortez, the notorious playboy—didn't sit well with me. It was clear they weren't the only men on the island. Their accounts were littered with photos of shirtless guys.

Alana wanted to get married there, but the requests were declined despite our offer to pay double. Now, it all made sense. Arianna would've stopped it. We weren't aware of her connection with the Cortez family until recently. Anger flared when I thought about Arianna now. While my mind said Arianna was innocent, I couldn't help but realize it didn't take long for her to jump into another man's bed.

My phone blared. "Hello."

"Brian, where are you? You're late again," my father complained.

"I'll be there in fifteen minutes." I disconnected the call. With a shaking breath, I started the car. Alana was right. Arianna was using me to get to her. She would never be the wife I wanted. No one in our social circle would accept or respect her. Meeting her and falling in love with her was a mistake.

Chapter 18

The wedding was perfect in every sense. Tears of joy streamed down my cheeks when Enrique kissed Chiara. The setting sun cast a golden shadow on the couple, and the photographers utilized the moment to capture the moments that would be remembered forever.

Warm lips graced my bare shoulder, and I turned to meet Orlando's stormy gaze. We moved aside, and I stayed by his side as he greeted the guests, introducing me to them.

The function was a blur, and my cheeks ached with all the smiling I'd been doing that evening. We shared our first dance together, and I couldn't help but admire how delectable he looked in his white suit.

"That was such a wonderful moment." Mike's mom burst into tears.

"It was." Orlando smiled down at his aunt.

"I'm so happy for you both." She hugged me. "Ari and Rosa are my darlings. Take good care of her, Orlando. I don't want to see any more tears in her eyes."

Orlando's face tightened. Mr. Frisby was right on time for the rescue. He pulled his wife away with a wink in our direction, and I felt Orlando's posture relaxing beside me.

"Sorry about that."

"It's okay."

When it was time for the dance, he led me to the dance floor. Our feet moved in rhythm, our bodies gently swaying. My skin tingled where he touched it. The memory of our previous dance surfaced, filling me with anticipation.

"Lavender suits you better," he murmured while his hand moved to rest above the curve of my ass.

"Mhmm. The other day, you said purple looked good on me."

"Do you want me to tell you the truth?"

"Yes."

"I think none of the colors do you justice," he claimed, making my head spin. Excitement bubbled in me. "You looked much better without any colors on you." His voice lowered, whispering the last part.

My body was instantly on fire, and my cheeks heated up. "You shouldn't talk like that."

"You wanted the truth, and I'm being honest."

When he twirled me, I took a much-needed breath before being pressed to his side again. "Your honesty should wait until we get somewhere private."

Orlando chuckled, and his lips brushed my forehead. "I'll be right back."

My gaze followed him, and I nodded when I saw Dean McAllister waving at him. I looked around and found my friends on the dance floor. Rosie waved at me, beckoning me over.

"You're glowing tonight, Rosie."

"No. Chiara is the star tonight."

"Can't disagree, but you look really great tonight," Jeff piped in.

I winked at Rosie, who laughed. "So, did you guys set a date?"

"No. I'm heading with Jeff to meet his parents."

"That's great."

"Hey, Ari, how about a dance?" Mike twirled me around, making me giggle.

"Sure."

It was once again like the old days. My evening was filled with laughter and fun. Weddings united families. Chiara's family members took their turns dancing with the bride and groom. Uncle Rick stepped out of his comfort zone and was dancing with Chiara's aunt while Grandpapa Cortez chatted with Chiara's grandma. Mike's parents waved at me and continued with their dance. They were always so much in love with each other.

When it was time to call it a night, I found myself alone in the room. Enrique had carried Chiara to their honeymoon suite in bridal style while the others whisked away their own partners. I didn't see Orlando for the rest of the night, and it shouldn't bother me. But I found myself mulling over it and couldn't help but think that he ditched me. *No. He wouldn't do that.*

With nothing to do and my brain wide awake, I tried to busy myself with removing my makeup and taking my time. When it didn't keep me occupied, I stepped into the shower stall and yanked the faucet. The hot water soothed my muscles, but there was no controlling my raging nerves. I didn't want to be alone tonight.

By the time my feet hit the soft carpeted floor of my room, my mind was made up. *I'm finding him.* Pulling on a short dress that flared at the hip, I dabbed on some cologne before locking the door to my room. *I'm a woman on a mission.*

Bare feet made no noise as I approached his room. My heart suddenly lurched, hand pausing in mid-air. What if he had company? I was quick to curb that thought. *Relax.* The knock was hesitant, and I almost turned, aborting the mission.

The door swung open, and he stood there, still wet from the shower. The towel hung dangerously low on his hips. Crap. Desire pooled in my belly and traveled south. Laughter wanted to bubble out. He wasn't expecting me. Did he really think he could ditch me like that?

"Hey, can't sleep?"

"I want you tonight, Orlando." I paused, allowing him to register my words, and stopped him before he objected or said anything to change my mind. "I expect nothing from this. I just want to forget. Everyone has company tonight, and I feel alone. I don't want to feel alone. Please, I want to know how it would feel to be wanted. I want to know…Orlando. Show me how it would feel to be loved by a man."

"Ari—"

I kissed him, pushing him away from the door, and kicked it closed. He staggered, taking me with him, when his back hit the mattress. Lust and desire were my driving force. I felt him open up to my seeking tongue, his hands running along my back.

A throaty moan left his lips when my hips ground against him. His cock was hard and pressed against my thigh. My hand slid between our bodies, stroking him, and he shuddered. I continued to kiss his neck, nipping his skin as his member twitched in my hand.

When he switched positions, I was caged between his broad frame and the mattress. His weight pressed down, allowing me to feel all the solid, muscular lines of his body. Our chests heaved, and our breathing grew heavy as his hands worked on removing my dress.

I wore no bra. When his eyes zeroed in on my hardened peaks, they were tingling with anticipation. And he didn't make me wait for long. His head dipped, taking one aching nipple in his mouth while his thumb and forefinger rolled the other. My back arched when his tongue rolled around my areola, sucking the tip.

Jolts of pleasure shot through me, igniting my primal need. I dug my fingers into his shoulder as my toes curled. My loud moan drifted around us. My eyes rolled to the back of my head as his attention turned to the other breast. Strong fingers slid beneath my underwear, exploring my womanhood. By the time his lips traveled past my navel, I was writhing with pleasure and anticipation.

"Orlando..."

His eyes locked with mine briefly, and the corners of his lips lifted. His strong hands tugged at my panties, removing them. Long, tan fingers traced my skin from hip to ankles. I was bare in front of him. It should've made me feel vulnerable, but it didn't. My heart raced, and my belly clenched.

Orlando's eyes darkened with lust as he licked his lips. A shudder ran through my body as his intention became clear. His fingers parted my folds, revealing more to his eyes. "You're so beautiful and wet." His voice was hoarse with need. One finger pressed on my clit, making my whole body jerk. My head tipped back against the mattress, and my teeth involuntarily bit my lower lip to control the moan.

One hand reached out, releasing my lip from my teeth. "I want to hear it." He pushed my legs apart with his broad shoulders and used them to keep my thighs open while his eyes drank in my sex. Then, without warning, he buried his face in my apex.

My hips jerked at the first brush of his tongue. The next few minutes had me writhing under his ruthless mouth, begging for mercy, and when he relented, a scream tore past my lips. The pleasure rendered me speechless, and I was panting hard when he climbed between my legs. A distant sound of something being torn reached my ears.

Body and mind, giddy with pleasure, I peered at him through half-hooded eyes when his erection pressed against my entrance. Then he sank deep, stretching my sex. I could feel every inch of him filling me as I gasped for breath. It felt so good. When he began to move, I was lost. My legs wrapped around his waist, holding him closer as his hands locked mine over my head. His lips claimed mine again, swallowing my moans.

Suddenly, Orlando pulled out of me and dashed into the bathroom, leaving my emotions in disarray. I blinked in confusion, wondering if I'd done something wrong. It didn't last long, maybe less than a minute, but I could tell he came too soon and was upset. *Maybe he just went to discard the condom?*

Disappointment washed over me. Why was I upset? This was just sex, wasn't it? I sat straight, trying to collect my jumbled thoughts. My body still pulsed with need. The remnants of pleasure still clung to my soft spot and made the skin tingle when I moved. Should I go in there? Why did he run away like that? Did I do something I wasn't supposed to do?

When he didn't come out, I decided to check on him. I shrugged on his shirt before going in. I could see him through the crack of the door. Orlando stood clutching the bathroom counter, his knuckles white with the pressure. The expression on his face was something I wasn't expecting. Pure disgust and anger coated his features, and it made me wonder if I was the reason for his disgust.

I watched him grab a bottle of pills from one of the cabinets. What was that for? Before I had time to comprehend, he opened the cap in a swift move, popping a pill into his hand.

"What are you doing?"

Orlando whirled around as shock replaced his anger. "Why are you here?" His voice rang with a tinge of anger, and I let it slide.

"What are those tablets for?"

"That's none of your business," he spat.

The fury in his voice caught me off guard. While I wanted to recoil and run away, I saw something else flash in his eyes. Hurt. I had to remind myself that he was like a wounded animal. Sometimes, you just had to risk a bite to tend to their injuries.

"It is in every sense my business since you left me hanging." I saw him flinch at the mention of his abrupt departure, and I grabbed the bottle, reading the prescription before he could stop me.

"Give it to me!" He snatched the bottle. "Get out."

I stood unmoving; the information I just read kept swirling in my mind as I locked my gaze on his. Sex stamina pills? Someone hurt his male ego, he told me. Did that have something to do with this? Did he believe he wasn't good enough?

"You don't need this pill."

"Don't test my patience, Arianna. Did you think you can ask me questions just because we're fooling around and fucked once?"

It stung. But the hurt in his eyes overrode the anger on his face. "No," I whispered. "But it matters when you resort to this pill to fuck me."

Orlando looked taken aback, but he was still brooding. It was as if he was expecting me to say something worse. "Leave, Arianna." His voice softened with hurt and defeat; his back turned to me.

"I won't."

"I'll leave, then."

I caught him before he could leave. "It doesn't matter how long you can fuck me. What matters is how you make me feel during and after."

His posture stiffened, but he didn't turn. It felt as if I understood the reason behind his hurt.

"You made me feel special and wanted," I continued. "It felt good to be wanted for once. Trust me, you don't need that." Tears blurred my vision.

"Arianna..."

"I'm not her, Orlando." My tears broke free, trickling down my chin. "I'm not her."

His demeanor changed, and he scooped me in his arms, his lips covering mine. My lungs expanded, breathing him in. I tasted his tears on his lips, and at that moment, something shifted within me.

What I felt for him wasn't just a leftover teenage crush. No, this was intense. More intense than the feelings I had for Brian. Thinking his name had no effect on me at that moment, which clarified everything.

My eyes rolled into my skull when Orlando plunged in without warning, claiming my body, this time without a barrier. He hoisted me onto the counter. With each thrust, his kiss deepened, consuming not just my body but my soul. I knew I had fallen for this man more deeply than I ever had for Brian.

I took what he offered and gave him everything I had. There wasn't a loser in this game. Orlando grunted, his hand going between us to my center of need. I threw my head back as his lips trailed down to my neck, my ass perched on the bathroom counter. He lowered his head, catching one of my nipples in his mouth, and every logical thought left my mind.

Chapter 19

When I woke up the next morning, Orlando wasn't in the bed. The clock showed 10:15 a.m. The delicious aroma of crispy bacon, toast, and scrambled eggs wafted to my nostrils. I turned to look at the hearty meal as a smile graced my lips.

An orchid with a note rested on top of a glass of water.

Arianna,

I'm leaving early for work. I'll call once I'm done here.

Orlando.

The note was simple. I appreciated his responsibility as warmth coated my insides. After the heart-warming breakfast and a quick shower, I was just pulling on my dress when it came to my mind that we had to leave today. Crap. I didn't want to leave yet.

Remembering I left my slippers in my room last night, I hurried to pack.

"I won!"

I was greeted by Rosie's squeal when I opened the door. The entire girls' group was here, including Chiara. The girls chuckled under their breath as I made my way toward them. They were packing my clothes.

"What are you doing here?" I asked Chiara. "I thought you wouldn't surface for another week or two."

Chiara rolled her eyes. "I'm not going anywhere. Besides, Enrique is arranging a ride for you guys. Orlando had to leave early and took the chopper."

"Oh."

"We knew you wouldn't be here, so we came to pack for you. But, man, was it worth it? Never in my nine lives have I thought I'd get to see you walking bow-legged. And that's how it feels to have a hot man in your bed." Rosie held her stomach, laughing hard.

"Shh...quiet, bish." I felt the familiar heat rush to my cheeks. "I'll give you a hundred dollars when we get home."

Rosalinda winked. "I'm so happy for you, Ari. But I don't want your money. In fact, I changed my mind. Make me the godmother of your baby with Orlando."

"What?" My eyes almost popped out of their sockets while Skyler and Chiara boomed with laughter.

"If that's the case, I'm calling dibs for the second kid." Skyler raised her arm.

"Hey, that's not fair. I'll get the third, then," Chiara said, pulling Skyler's arm down.

"In fact, I think we should all try for a baby at the same time. If we succeed, then our babies will grow up together and be best friends, just like us," Rosie said in a dreamy voice.

"Girls!" I yelped. "It was just one night."

"Yeah, first of the many to come." Chiara wiggled her brows.

"I don't even know if I'll see him again. He's leaving for his business trip this week." I could hear the complaint in my voice.

"So what? You can always talk to him."

"I don't know." I sighed. That nagging doubt was back again. What if Orlando didn't want to see me after this? What if it was nothing more than a fling for him? *It's not true.*

"Hmm…let's see, did he hold you after you did the deed?" Chiara asked.

"Um…yes."

"Did he say you felt good? I mean, was he vocal about his desire for you?" Skyler asked.

"Yes." I bit my lower lip, wondering what they were getting at.

"Was it a one-night thing, or did you have a repeat this morning?" Rosie sounded like a detective, and it made me laugh.

"We had a repeat." Now I was blushing. He made love to me again in the early hours of the morning.

"Did he kiss you after each time? Or did he do anything else that felt intimate?" Skyler asked.

I thought for a moment. "He kissed me a few times and rested his forehead on mine the other times, staying like that for a bit."

"This is an intimate question," Rosie drawled. "Did he pull out immediately, or did he stay in you while he held you?"

"Um…" That was very intimate, but there were no secrets between us. It had been that way for many years. "He stayed in." If you didn't count the first time.

"You got yourself a keeper, Ari. Cheers!" Rosie declared, and the others beamed.

"How do you know all this?"

"Experience and information we gained by talking to other women." Chiara shrugged.

I hoped they were right. Now, if only Orlando would see it that way.

***

At first glance, nothing much had changed since I last left this place. But on close observation, I noticed the new additions. The lawns were mowed, and new decorative plants had occupied the place of the old ones. It wasn't a surprise. How easily they replaced things. The artificial fountain now held a brand-new statue of Venus.

The taxi drove past the garden that now sported new flowers and ornamental plants. A team of professionals were buzzing with their equipment.

Regret filled me when I stepped into my parents' home. Coming here was a mistake. But I needed someplace to stay while planning my next move. I wasn't eager to meet anyone. However, when I stepped inside, I bumped into someone, and my eyes almost bulged out, seeing my mirror image.

That bitch. Anger flared in my veins. What the fuck was wrong with her? I wanted to blast and push at her, but I knew how she'd react. She'd stagger back with crocodile tears in her eyes. My good-for-nothing parents would support her, saying she was just trying to mend her relationship with me.

When I changed my hair color to not resemble her anymore, she now stood before me with a new hair color that matched mine. Brian hovered behind her, and when our eyes met, they held. It was as if he was apologizing for her behavior. The crestfallen look on his face caught me by surprise.

With a shake of my head, I steered clear of her and climbed the stairs to my room.

"Miss Swanson!"

My feet stopped out of habit, and I turned to see the wedding planner.

"We were waiting for you, actually." She laughed nervously. The planner, in her late twenties, had a friendly demeanor that stopped me from snapping at her. "Your bridesmaid gown is here. If you could—"

"She is not a bridesmaid." Andrea, one of her bitches, came forward. My sister just stood there, silent. Her friends always did the dirty work for her.

Oh, so they were stationed here forever now. Didn't they have homes? As for the bridesmaid part, I rolled my eyes. I never would've played the role, anyway. Why bother when it held no meaning to you or the bride?

"Oh, but here..."

"Maria, as I said, she doesn't want to be a bridesmaid. Her schedule is too busy fucking elite bachelors to attend her sister's wedding."

Fucking bitch!

"And what about you, Andrea? When will you ever grow tired of being my sister's bitch?"

Her face distorted, and I noticed my parents entering the scene. *Very well.*

"You—"

"Does Alana know that you used to fuck her high school sweetheart while they were dating? Oh, she wouldn't know that since she was too busy keeping up with her grades." I continued, enjoying the shocked expression on her face. Her mouth gaped like a fish out of water. "What I do and who I date is none of your business." My eyes narrowed at her. "Stay out of it. And that goes to everyone here." With that said, I turned and left without a second look.

Coming here was a mistake. Once again, the insecurities and worry were beginning to crawl their way back into my mind. Being in the same room with them was the last thing on my planner. I didn't bother going down for dinner. Instead, I munched on a granola bar while browsing through my Instagram page, blocking *her, him,* and their friends.

I was about to block his number from my phone contacts when the message came in.

Brian: We need to talk.

I ignored it.

Brian: Please...It's urgent.

My fingers hovered over the keypad for a moment.

Arianna: There is nothing to talk about.

His reply was instant.

Brian: Meet me at the park. Our usual place at 12 a.m.

I blocked his contact and tossed the phone aside. The nerve of him. What did he want to talk about? It was over. He was getting married in less than a week.

My mind drifted to Orlando. He hadn't called yet, and he didn't respond to my calls or messages. *Maybe he's still busy.*

I missed him already. The two weeks in New Ikandas changed my life forever. It made me realize many things I hadn't given a thought about before. The first thing I learned was to love myself more.

Mike and Skyler invited me to stay at their place until the wedding, but I politely declined, saying I wanted some time for myself, which was true. I looked around the room I'd had since childhood. Alana was never willing to share her space with me, so we were given separate rooms when we turned two.

Growing up, I never understood why she wanted first place in everything she did. We never were the sisters we should've been. She'd proven that on our fourth birthday by pushing me into the pool. The memory has been etched in my mind forever. I approached her group and asked to be included in the game they were playing.

She'd called me mean names my childish brain couldn't comprehend and pushed me into the pool, ruining my dress. The only words I understood then were, "I hate you. I wish I never had a sister." Still, no one scolded her that day.

A lone tear escaped my eyes. *Whoa, there...aren't we supposed to get past this? You decided to cut ties with them and move on, remember?* Yes. I swore never to shed a tear over them again, and now I was going back to square one. With a determined sigh, I took the phone and called Rosie.

"Hey, bish, what are you doing?" she greeted. I could feel the laughter in her voice. She was happy.

"Nothing. What about you?"

"We're shopping." That explained the loud noises from her line.

"Okay. Carry on, then. I'll talk to you later."

"Are you okay?"

"Yeah, just bored. That's all."

"I'm in the Linnesse City Mall. Why don't you join us?"

I contemplated that for a moment. "Nah. I'd like to stay in."

"Okay, then. Call me if you need to talk, okay?"

"Okay."

Getting up from the bed, I went to the closet and decided to pack my things. A few minutes into the job, I realized I had many things that reminded me of him. Without another thought, I began tossing his gifts and cards into a box. My heart dropped, and my hand itched to open them. See them one last time. No. *It won't bring any good.* I kept the dresses and jewelry he bought for me and packed them in a separate bag to put it in a charity box.

A few hours later, I stopped when my back ached. There were so many things left to be sorted. I had a habit of keeping everything, and the boxes I had were now overflowing with items I never had any use for.

My back groaned in protest. I checked the time, and it was past one a.m. After thinking for a moment, I decided to take the garbage out and then take a shower before bed. A quick glance at my cell phone told me there were no calls or messages from Orlando yet.

It shouldn't bother me. He was a busy man, and it wasn't like I was his priority. That thought hurt. No expectations. But didn't I cross that line already? Over the two weeks, I had not only moved on from my ex but also had fallen head over heels for my crush.

When I exited the room with two garbage bags, there was no one outside. It was a ten-minute walk to the main gate and then another five to the dumpster. Usually, the servants did the job. A grunt left my mouth when I ran into someone.

"Arianna, I thought you'd never come." His voice was relieved.

"I'm taking the garbage out." My legs didn't stop their march, and a strong hand took one of the bags from mine. I continued toward my destination, with him following close behind.

"There's a lot I need to tell you, starting with how sorry I am."

His words fell on deaf ears. The warm breeze fiddled with my hair where it had escaped from the band. I clutched the bag tighter in my arms, half dragging and half carrying it.

"A sorry won't rectify what I've done to you. I was forced to choose her, and my parents would've never accepted you."

My eyes rolled. He would get no response from me. Did he realize he was helping me to remove himself from my life? The bags he carried contained the worthless gifts among the other things he'd bought for me.

"I should've fought harder for us. And I should've—"

"Do you need any help, sir?" one of the security guards volunteered.

"Sure. Can you carry this one out, please?" I handed him my bag.

"Certainly, ma'am."

"Ari—"

"Thanks for helping, Brian. My sister must be waiting for you." I turned and walked away without another look.

Chapter 20

"Arianna, wait!"

What did he want now? No matter how much I avoided him, he was determined to get me alone. Last night, he knocked at my door until I threatened to scream and wake everyone in the house. My heart used to ache for him. Now, the only emotion I felt for him was disgust.

"What the fuck do you want?"

His handsome features cringed. "Please...I want to talk."

"I told you there is nothing left to say."

"There is...please, let me explain." His expression was pained. Though it shouldn't bother me, it tugged at my heartstrings. "All I'm asking for is a chance to talk. Please..."

My fingers reached to massage my temples as I considered his plea. "Okay, and after that, you should stop bugging me."

"I promise."

"We'll talk tonight."

"The same spot."

"Fine." I didn't wait to see the relief flooding his face. My thoughts were on Orlando. His cell phone had been switched off for the past three days, and it had been driving me crazy. I was restless and restrained myself from calling Enrique. *Did he leave already?* I thought he'd at least say goodbye. I continued to pace the confines of my room.

My phone blared, interrupting my thoughts. "Hey, Rosie."

"You're shutting me out again."

"I'm not."

"Bitch, you didn't respond to my calls or messages since last night."

"It slipped my mind. I've been busy."

"Busy doing what?"

An exhausted sigh left my lungs, and I plopped on my bed. "I'm moving out after the wedding."

"That's good news. Need any help?"

"Nah... I'm almost done."

"Did you speak to Orlando?"

"His phone is switched off." She'd have caught the defeat in my voice.

"Oh, I'm sorry, Ari. It must be because of his tight schedule. Do you want me to check with someone?"

"No," I said quickly. I didn't want anyone to worry. This was expected. I mean, I did tell him I expected nothing, didn't I? Pain filled my chest. The familiar ache spread in the cavity of my ribcage. Once, it ached for someone who didn't deserve it.

"Oh, baby. I'm coming now."

"No. It's all right. I'm fine."

"I'm on my way."

I ended the call, defeated. The truth was that I needed someone and was just trying to act tough. Half an hour later, my door burst open, and my bed dipped. Rosie didn't speak as she hugged me. We lay there in comfortable silence as her fingers massaged my head. It was a habit between us. She'd been more of a sister than Alana would ever be.

"Orlando wouldn't avoid you without reason. You know that, don't you?" Her gentle whisper caressed my ears.

"I know, but I can't help feeling like this."

Her hold on me tightened. "Love hurts. Whether you're too happy or too sad, love is painful."

I couldn't agree more. "Do you know she changed her hair color? She looks like me now."

"What the...?"

"I know." A deep sigh left my lips, and the weight once again settled in my heart. "I blocked them all from my social media accounts."

"Why would she want to color her hair?"

"I wish I knew, Rosie. I'm gonna change again, and this time, she'll never get a glimpse. Sometimes, I feel like I'm a fugitive running from something. You know, changing my looks and all."

"Trust me, girl. Running from the FBI and Interpol sounds much better than this." Her brows creased in thought. "But seriously, why would she want to steal your identity?"

"Brian wants to talk to me."

"About what?"

"I don't know. He's persistent and won't give me a moment's peace."

"That bastard. I'm gonna have a talk with him."

"No, Rosie. I told him I'll meet him tonight. Whatever it is, I'll make sure there's nothing left between us after this."

"Do you want me to stay?"

"Not really. It's nothing I can't handle."

"Okay." Her gaze narrowed, and her teeth gripped her lower lip, something she did when she was deep in thought. "Perhaps there's trouble in paradise. Does he want you back? Is that why she's trying to impersonate you? To keep him?"

"As reasonable as it sounds, it's sick."

"That it is."

Is that why he wants to meet me? Does he want me back?

***

"What did you want to talk about?" There was no one at the park at this time of night. I shouldn't have come. But I had to end this tonight.

"Look, Arianna. I messed up. I know that now. I should've fought for our love, but I didn't," he pleaded desperately.

"Why are you saying this now?" He made his choice. And it was *her*.

"Because I don't want to lose you, Arianna."

What the hell? Did he even realize what he had just said?

"You already lost me, Brian."

"Hear me out, please. I lied to you. Alana was the first one I met. My parents wanted us to get married. But then, one day, I bumped into you and got intrigued."

I stood silently as he ranted.

"I wanted to get to know you better. I fell in love with you and even broke up with Alana."

My suspicion was right. They knew each other before he met me. He was going behind her back. "So, you were seeing each other."

"Kind of."

"There can be only one answer to this question, Brian. It's either yes or no."

"Yes."

"So, you were sleeping together."

His head bowed, confirming my accusation. "Yes."

"Okay. What you both did or do is none of my business. I don't want someone to see us together and assume something. I should go."

"Please..." he pleaded, clutching at my arm. "I love you, Arianna. I should've been truthful with you from the beginning. I've realized my mistake now."

"Let me go, Brian." I tried to pry his hands off me, only for him to tighten the hold.

"No. Please." His eyes teared up. "Hear me out, please. I was going to talk to my parents. But then I saw your party photos."

My cheeks heated up, remembering the embarrassing paparazzi photos.

"When I arrived, my parents showed me the photos and said how disgusting they were. They said it is why I should never associate with you now that I'm going to marry Alana."

"Good. You listened to your parents." I tried to leave again.

"I had no choice. Alana is pregnant."

It shouldn't have affected me, but I'd have been lying if I said it didn't. It confirmed he lied about their breakup, even now. We dated for five months. They were fucking each other while he was dating me, and it made my stomach sick.

"She forced me to break it off with you. I don't want her. I want you. No matter how hard she tried, she will never be you. Let's go somewhere and get married. We'll leave this all behind and start fresh."

"Do you even hear yourself? That's the most horrendous thing I ever heard. What about your parents? What about the company and its reputation?" The new edge of my anger knew no bounds. I felt disgusted for even looking at him.

"It can all go to hell, for all I care. I can't live without you. I realize that now. Look, I don't care about your photos, and I don't care that you cheated on me because I was doing the same to you. Let's forget everything and start fresh."

"What the hell are you talking about? I never cheated on you." My blood boiled. How could he accuse me of something like this? "I don't love you anymore, Brian. We shouldn't even be here like this."

"Alana...hear me out, please."

"I'm not *Alana*." Brian stilled. A sigh left my lips as I contemplated his words. Did he even understand what he'd said? "We're over, Brian. Nothing you say will change the outcome of this meeting." I straightened my shoulders and locked my gaze with his.

I was about to leave, but he pulled me closer, capturing my lips. I yelped in surprise as he deepened the kiss, filled with heat and passion. My lips moved against my wishes before I stilled. While the kiss roused all my warm memories, it was wrong in every sense. It didn't feel right anymore.

I pushed him away with a force that surprised him. Before my mind could decide what I was about to do was right, my palm connected with his cheek with a loud crack. A stinging sensation spread across my palm as my skin reddened.

Brian clutched his cheek with wide eyes. His jaw went slack. "Arianna..."

"Don't." My hiss silenced him, and he took a step back. I'd never been so furious before, not even when he betrayed me. "I feel ashamed for even falling in love with you, Brian." I didn't care how loud I was being. I had to get it off my chest. "There is no place for you in my heart anymore. You've betrayed me and didn't even have the decency to break up with me before you went on one knee in front of her."

My chest rose and fell with every heavy breath. "Alana and I might never have a friendly relationship. She might have backstabbed me more times than I can count. But I'll never, ever do the same to any woman, even if it is Alana."

"Ari—"

I raised my hand, stopping him. "You are going to become my brother-in-law. My sister's husband and the father of my niece or nephew. Did you ever think of that child?"

"I..."

"You didn't. You see, Brian, we would've never worked out. I was smitten with your charms. But eventually, I would've seen right through your façade and left you. I'm glad it ended the way it did."

Brian hung his head. His shoulders slumped. If it was a few months ago, I would've been there, holding him. But now he only irritated me.

"You deserve each other. Go home to my sister, Brian. I hope you'll treat her better than me and love your child the way it deserves to be loved. Please don't ever try to see me or talk to me after this. Whatever we had, it ends right here. And I thank you for everything. I was happier during the first few months I was with you, and your betrayal helped me realize there are better things in this world. I wish you a good life."

When I turned, my chest felt light, and a smile crept over my lips. This time, he didn't stop me.

My breathing grew heavier as the distance between me and Brian grew. It hurt, and tears badly wanted out. But I refused to cry. He didn't deserve my tears. I rubbed my lips furiously, trying to get rid of the way his kiss made me feel—*dirty.*

Fuck!

How did he even think I'd go with him after everything?

My sister was pregnant. I couldn't believe it. She knew he was seeing me behind her back, and she let him. How sick was that? *Why?* She could've fought me. Told me he belonged to her. *Why?*

People say you should make no decision while you are angry or sad. But I had to decide. I'd leave tomorrow after the wedding and never look back. My shoulders straightened as the thought took hold. I lost any hope I had for my family. There was no point in trying. If they wanted to see me as a Swanson, they would have done that already.

Sadness weighed down my heart. What did I ever do for them to hate me so much? Would they have hated Alana if she was the one who partied instead of me?

A sudden yelp escaped my mouth, and my body was pinned against something my mind registered as a car. Warm lips encased mine as a familiar scent of cologne clouded my senses. His mouth swallowed my relieved sobs, and soon, my back pressed against the soft leather.

"Orlando..." I couldn't hide my surprise when he closed the door to his car. I thought he already left the country. "How did—"

His lips silenced me before I could complete the sentence. I opened to his seeking tongue and melted under his skillful hands. There was urgency in his movements, and I loved it. His lips sucked and nipped mine.

Orlando was already between my legs and had my dress bundled up above my hips. Frantic fingers moved lower.

A gasp of pleasure left my lips when he entered me. "I missed you," I heard him say before he kissed me again. His hands cupped my breast over my dress. His hips thrust in a fervent rhythm as his other hand gripped my ass, adjusting his position to allow him deeper than before. Our combined moans filled the confined space as the car rocked, matching his thrusts.

The familiar pressure built in my lower region, spreading the pleasure-filled vibration to the tips of my toes. Orlando vocalized his pleasure as our breathing grew heavier.

His lips released mine to shower me with wet kisses along my neck and the valley of my breasts. "You feel so good."

"Oh, Orlando..."

"Say my name again," he said hoarsely.

"Orlando..."

"Yes...I love my name on your lips." His hand on my breast slipped between our bodies, finding the center of my need.

"Orlando...I..." I didn't know what I wanted to say. My thoughts were haywire.

"Arianna!" He came with my name on his lips, his cock twitching within me. The pressure hadn't been released from my body yet, and my hips arched on their own. He continued to stroke me until I cried out his name along with my release. His chest pressed against mine as he rested his forehead on mine. Our breath mingled.

"I thought you left already." My voice wavered. I couldn't thank him enough for being here when I needed him the most.

"I wouldn't leave without telling you."

"Your mobile was switched off," I accused.

"I'm sorry. Isabela was calling non-stop, and I locked it in my office drawer."

"Oh." I thought he had sorted that out. There were many things I didn't know.

"You're cute when you do that." He pecked my lips, making me laugh.

"Orlando, what are we?"

"I don't know," he sighed. "No expectations, remember?"

I nodded, closing my eyes. *No expectations.* Then why couldn't I help wanting more?

He paused for a moment. "You are my friend, and I trust you more than anyone, that much I can tell you now."

"That sounds better." I wanted to voice my fear of losing him, but I stayed quiet.

He isn't ready yet.

Chapter 21

A deep sigh escaped the confines of my lungs when Orlando allowed me to get up, and both of us adjusted our clothes. "Stay with me tonight," he murmured as he looked at me intently. "Or I can stay with you."

"Why?"

"Is that question necessary?" His brows rose. "I'm not done with you yet."

A smile crept on my lips as I watched him climb into the driver's seat. I was giddy with excitement as I slipped between the front seats to sit in the passenger seat. "Your apartment is an hour away. I prefer you in my room tonight."

"Impatient, I see."

"Can you blame me?"

Orlando's free hand held mine as we drove back to my parents' home.

"How did you find me here?"

"I was coming to see you. When I saw you crossing the road, I followed."

"You saw."

A slight pause before he responded. "I did."

"He'd been pressuring me to meet and said he wanted to talk. He said it was urgent."

Orlando raised my hand to his lips, pressing them on my wrist. "You don't have to explain anything, Arianna. I followed you and stayed in earshot to make sure you were okay."

"I wanted you to know."

Orlando smiled, turning the car toward my...*their* home. It wasn't my home anymore. I was never welcomed there. Bringing Orlando with me was a bold decision, but I didn't give a flying fuck what they'd think. Perhaps I'd raise their blood pressure for a night before leaving them for good. *For my own good.*

Everyone whirled around, freezing in position when I entered, hand in hand with Orlando. My eyes locked with Alana's bloodshot ones. *What happened?* Her tear-stained face registered in my mind first. She clutched her phone tightly, and I noticed the shock on her face. *Or is it surprise?* She and her friends were dressed for bed. *What's going on? Why is everyone down here at this time of night?*

"Mr. Cortez?" My dad was the first one to step forth with a questioning gaze.

"Hello, Mr. Swanson." Orlando's tone was clipped. His gaze swept through the room, analyzing each face before settling on my dad. "Arianna, why don't you bring your overnight bag? I'll wait here."

Confusion clouded my mind, and I looked around, wondering what he saw that changed his mind.

"Arianna..." Orlando nudged me.

"Huh! Yeah, sure. I'll be right back." I felt their gazes following me when I climbed the stairs. It helped that I didn't unpack after my return from Ikandas. I walked over to my closet, where I had dumped my bags earlier, and picked them up before going back down.

"I'll take them." Orlando took a bag from me. "See you at the wedding, Mr. Swanson." He nodded at my dad before taking my hand in his other hand.

"Sure." My dad's unsure voice followed us out.

"Something isn't right," Orlando said as he opened the passenger door for me. "Perhaps, they—" He stopped mid-sentence and climbed in the driver's seat.

"Perhaps what?"

Orlando shrugged. "It's just a hunch I have, but I feel like your sister might have found out you were meeting Brian tonight."

It made sense. Why else would everyone be there now?

"Thanks for getting me out of there. I was planning to leave right after the wedding."

"I'll get Mike to move the rest of your things to your new apartment. You can stay with me until then."

My eyes snapped to his face. *Why the hell did that sound like 'move in with me?' Shut it, Ari.*

When we arrived at his apartment an hour later, he used the spare key to open the door. "Miriam is the housekeeper here. She looks after Boxer and my home," he said while holding the door wide for me to enter. "Boxer sleeps with her."

"Okay." I swallowed the smile and averted my face. Excitement bubbled within me.

"Do you want anything to eat?"

"No. I'm not hungry."

"Good." I giggled when he pulled me toward him and buried his face in my neck. "I'm hungry for you."

"What are you doing?" I asked as he moved us further into his room before kicking the door shut.

"You ask as if you don't know already." He nipped at my earlobe. "I told you I'm not done with you yet."

"What's your plan?" My voice grew huskier.

"You'll find out soon." He smirked, pushing me on his mattress. I scooted back, allowing him space.

"Orlando..." His name whooshed past my lips when he pulled me by my legs to the edge of his bed, resting his hands on my inner thighs.

"Did you think I'd leave like that?" I could only gasp when the cold air hit my skin. "You look delectable tonight, Ari..." His lips brushed my skin, trailing feather-soft kisses from my knee to my upper thighs. "Are you tired?" His warm breath fanned my center.

"No." My breathing was growing harsher with anticipation. Sleep was far from my thoughts.

"Good, because I don't have any intention to let you sleep tonight."

Fuck! I didn't know if this moment could get any sexier. I liked this side of him. His hands ran along the length of my legs, his fingers massaging my calf as he removed my shoes. I watched him with hooded eyes as he took his time.

My throat moved to swallow when my shoes hit the floor. The tips of his fingers continued to feel my skin.

Teasing.

Tracing.

Rubbing.

My toes curled, and my eyes wanted to roll into my skull when his fingers reached my inner thighs. The sound of my breathing grew heavier as he continued to remove each piece of my clothing. My anticipation grew with his everlasting patience. Soon, his lust-filled gaze devoured my bare body.

"Move to the center of the bed, Arianna," he commanded thickly, making me shiver.

His broad frame hovered over me. Removing his striped tie, he bound my hands to the headboard. Fuck. Wetness pooled down there, and my chest heaved. My center throbbed with need, and I rubbed my thighs together.

Soft music played in the background, and the lights dimmed. I saw him tossing a remote aside before shrugging off his coat. He then continued to remove his clothes, teasing me with a smirk. The dim lights illuminated his sculpted torso, and his muscles flexed with his movements. When he turned, my breath hitched. His erection glistened with his pre-cum.

Orlando climbed onto the bed and spread my thighs. His lips quirked.

"So wet and ready."

I sucked in a sharp breath, trying not to moan. His fingers traced the outline of my sex, parting the wet folds.

"You're so beautiful, Arianna. I've dreamed of this for years."

What?

Before I could think, his index finger plunged in, making me moan louder. His thumb circled my clit, spreading my wetness around. He lifted his fingers to his mouth, licking off my essence, which caused me to moan. "You taste like honey melons." My hands gripped the headboard. His head dipped between my thighs, and he ran his nose along my sex. My hips arched, hoping he'd get my intention, and he relented.

It took only a few strokes of his tongue to set me off. He continued to lick through my orgasm, sucking my clit and pumping his fingers in and out. A cry of pleasure left my lips as pressure built again.

"Orlando..." Hips shook. *Can't take any more.* "Please..."

His tongue increased the pressure on my aching bud, sending me over the cliff for the third time that night. My thighs closed, trying to shy away from his seeking mouth. "Please...N-need you now."

His head lifted, chin wet with my essence. He wiped his mouth and reached into the drawer, pulling out a condom. I watched him roll it down his length and position himself at my entrance. His eyes met mine and held as he plunged in.

"Ah!"

My legs wrapped around his hips as he began to thrust in a steady rhythm, slowly at first. Large hands cupped my breasts, kneading them gently and rolling the hard nipples between his fingers. I could only moan as he moved to suck one of the nipples into his hot mouth.

He sucked, licked, and nipped. It was overwhelming. *Too much pleasure.* The pressure was building again. He paused briefly, adjusting his position so his cock slid over my clit with each thrust.

I cried out his name when the fourth climax hit harder. I gasped for breath as he came with a grunt. His forehead rested on mine as we recovered. When he pulled out and walked to the washroom, I tried to catch my breath. He soon returned with a washcloth, cleaning me, once again taking his time. By the time he was done, my body was tuned for another round.

When I thought he was going to release my hands, he simply flipped me and pulled my hips so I was on all fours in front of him. Warm hands traced the length of my spine before his lips followed. And I knew he was just starting. *Oh, God!*

***

Brian Schultz

Trying to convince Arianna was a mistake. I should've seen this coming. But I was tired of living with Alana while wishing it was *her.* My love-struck brain was finally ready to overlook her past and take that step, but she brushed it off. My cheek stung, and her words were like knives to my heart. I had a baby on the way.

I hoped Alana didn't notice my absence. When I slipped in through the main door, I froze.

"Where have you been?" Her accusing gaze pinned me in place. Everyone, including her parents and friends, was there.

"I went for a walk."

"With whom?"

My gaze narrowed, and I found my phone in her grip. "Alone."

"You're lying! Dad, I know he went to see her. I checked her room. She's not there."

"I don't know what you're talking about." I was in no mood for this conversation, and she had no business with my phone.

"Liar! I saw your messages to her. You're cheating on me again."

"I'm not cheating on you."

"Then what the hell is this?" She showed me the messages I sent to Arianna. "You were tailing her this whole week. You—"

"We're getting married tomorrow, Alana. I thought maybe I could talk some sense into her," I lied through my teeth. "We're family, and we're going to see each other a lot." She'd rejected me, and I was stuck with Alana now. I was a fool to even think she'd see reason if I explained. Everything went wrong, and deep in my heart, I knew she wasn't the one to blame.

"You're lying."

"No. You're being paranoid. I don't understand your need to know where I am every second of the day."

"Then where is Arianna?"

"Enough." Mr. Swanson intervened. "Alana, I agree with Brian. You shouldn't be too hard on him."

"Your father is right, sweetie. This isn't the first time this has happened. You know your sister. Brian was trying to do what you always wanted to do," her mother added.

"And, in my opinion, you both should just stop trying to make her see reason," Mr. Swanson continued. "She never listens to anyone, and it's time we put a stop to this nonsense."

Her mother's shoulders slumped.

"She has caused nothing but trouble for this family. Arianna is no longer welcome here. After the wedding, I'll ask her to leave. Until then, I ask you all to focus on the wedding."

This isn't right. "Mr. Swanson, she's your daughter too. You should all sit with her and talk this out. I think you should give her a chance."

"We've given her enough chances, Brian. Everyone, go back to the bed, please."

My jaw clenched. There was nothing I could do. I knew their relationship was strained. But they weren't giving her a chance. This was all because of me. Arianna wouldn't be out on the street if it wasn't for me.

"We'll talk later." He dismissed us, and my disapproving gaze locked with Alana's briefly before I turned and walked into our room, which was on the ground floor.

"Dad, she's trying to steal him away from me." Her accusing voice reached my ears.

"She won't do a thing to you, sweetie. You must rest. We—" His words cut off. "Mr. Cortez?"

Cortez?

"Hello, Mr. Swanson." I didn't recognize the voice. I peeked through the crack of the door to see who it was. Orlando Cortez, the CEO of the Cortez empire, stood with her. I recognized him from the

Instagram pictures she shared. "Arianna, why don't you bring your overnight bag? I'll wait here."

Where did he come from? We were alone in the park. Did she call him? I thought he was just another fling. Is that why she didn't want me anymore?

Arianna frowned as she glanced at everyone in the living room. She wouldn't know the drama that went down here only a few seconds earlier.

"Arianna..." He nudged her.

"Huh! Yeah, sure. I'll be right back."

She climbed the stairs as my heart thudded against my ribs. *Why would she leave with him?*

"I wasn't expecting you," Henry, my father-in-law-to-be, said. I could sense his discomfort. Had Arianna returned alone, the situation would have been different. While I wasn't happy about his presence here, it worked in my favor.

"I came to see my girlfriend. Looks like it isn't the right time."

Girlfriend? Orlando did not date. So, the newspapers were right. They were together. My grip on the door handle tightened. I looked at Alana, who was gaping at our unexpected guest.

"Of course not. You're welcome here anytime." Henry looked at the others. "It's just surprising. I mean, um...you and my daughter." His laugh was nervous. He ran a hand through his hair. "Should've guessed when you refused to rent the Cortez estate."

"Arianna had nothing to do with the venue, Mr. Swanson. She doesn't run my business, I do. Besides, the venue was booked on the date you'd requested."

I knew he was talking about Enrique's wedding. The media swooned over the wedding photos. They also wrote how beautiful

Orlando's date looked. A magazine even claimed the Cortez empire would soon announce another wedding.

Arianna never mentioned anything about the Cortezes before. It was evident she knew the family. The photos from the wedding were proof enough. Then, something clicked in my mind.

Pulling out my phone, I swiftly searched on Google. My gaze skimmed through the pages, finally finding the connection. The Frisby family. My eyes widened with recognition. Her friend Michael Frisby was Orlando's cousin. That made sense now.

"Oh," I heard Henry say and looked up to see Arianna descending the stairs with her bags.

Orlando took one from her. "I'll take them. See you at the wedding, Mr. Swanson." He nodded at my future father-in-law before taking her hand in his free hand.

"Sure." Mr. Swanson's surprised voice followed them as I stood dumbfounded by the door.

What just happened? The way they held hands flashed in my mind. I didn't fail to notice her tousled hair or swollen lips. My anger flared. We were dating for six months, but she never allowed me to do anything past the kisses. Now they were fucking.

Their photos surfaced in my mind. Arianna wasn't who she claimed to be. Henry paid millions to the paparazzi every year to keep those photos from decorating the front page of the newspapers. Alana was right about her sister. She was just an opportunist, I decided. I was no one compared to Orlando.

She was also a good actress. She had fooled me into believing she was different.

I quickly slipped into the bathroom when I noticed Alana approaching the room. My mind was in turmoil. *You're a fool, Brian.*

I should just stick with Alana and stop worrying about *her*. It wouldn't do any good to my relationship with Alana if I was still hung up on her.

"Brian..." Alana called.

"Yes?" I sounded calm as I stripped, acting casual.

"I'm sorry about earlier."

"It's all right."

"No. It isn't all right. I should've trusted you." She sounded sincere.

"It's okay, Alana. Why don't you go to bed?" I sighed, changing into my nightwear.

"Tell me you forgive me."

"I forgive you."

When I opened the door, she was standing with tear-filled eyes. As much as I hated those tears, they also tugged at my heartstrings. "I love you." She stepped forward, burying her face in my chest.

"I love you too." My hand rested on her stomach. I had a baby to look forward to. With a tight smile, I led her to the bed.

Tomorrow will be a new day.

Chapter 22

S unlight streamed through the maple-colored curtains. I stretched under the sheets, relishing the soft texture caressing my bare skin. Orlando was missing from the bed. He was an early riser, unlike me.

A tray of food and flowers greeted me. *How can I not fall in love with this man?* My body ached deliciously when I hopped out of bed and walked to the bathroom.

I smiled to myself at the memories of last night's events. A deep chuckle had rumbled out of his chest when he flipped me on my stomach. His hand caressed my tattooed ass cheek, giving it a squeeze. His chuckle soon turned into full-blown laughter.

Why wouldn't he laugh? The tattoo consisted of a dark-colored dick with thick red letters reading "fuck me harder." The reason I always covered my bottom with modest underwear.

His hand had given a tap, making it bounce. "Those words are encouraging." He'd caressed the flesh before slipping his hands inside my dripping folds. The slow, torturous caress had driven me crazy. Orlando was like a man on a mission.

Shoving aside the thoughts that had the goosebumps erupt on my skin, I yanked the shower on. Hot water cascaded around me, washing away the remnants of last night. Rosie's face flashed in my mind. She'd be worried sick, and she would want an update on Brian.

The shower was quick, and I draped a towel around my body before stepping out. Strong hands picked me up, twirling me around. "What are you doing?" My giggle couldn't be helped. Orlando was already pulling me to the bed when his lips found my neck, kissing the soft spot there.

"I'm kissing you."

"I know that. Aren't you working today?"

"Nope. I took a day off to be your date."

"My date?"

"You have a wedding to attend, don't you?"

"Oh, yeah, that. I didn't know you were coming."

"Mhmm…" He continued to kiss my shoulder, earning a contented sigh from me.

Rosie's face popped into my mind again. "Could you pass me my phone, please?"

"Sure." He handed me the phone that was on the table without taking his lips off my skin, and I sent a quick text to Rosie, informing her that I was with Orlando.

"I'll miss you."

His gaze lifted to meet mine. The coldness in his gray eyes was now replaced with warmth. "I'll miss you too."

"Will you call?"

"I'll try."

"Okay." I averted my gaze to mask the hurt. *No expectations.*

His finger hooked under my chin, lifting my face to meet his gaze. "I'll be traveling around Europe, and I don't know if the time difference will work in our favor."

"Oh."

He bent, capturing my lips in a soft kiss. "What are you wearing?"

"I haven't decided yet."

He continued to pepper kisses along my skin as his hands curled around my waist. "You smell good."

"That must be your body wash I just used."

Orlando chuckled. He'd been smiling a lot these days, and I liked it. "I love your smile." My fingers traced his lips, which he kissed before sucking one into his mouth.

"And I love yours."

"We won't make it to the wedding on time if we don't stop this now."

"It's at three in the afternoon. We have enough time."

"Orlando..." I whispered. The need was growing under my skin, and his lips were there, silencing it.

***

When we reached the wedding venue—the garden of the Swanson residence—the bridal march was about to start. We slipped silently into one of the rows. Many heads turned toward us, which we ignored.

Brian had cleaned up well, as always, wearing a gray tux. His eyes followed us and averted as soon as the bridal march began. Why was I here again? I could've chosen to skip it. But I attended because I didn't want him to think I was weak. He used me and played with my emotions, leaving me scarred.

Orlando's fingers laced with mine as his lips broke into a soft smile reserved for me. It made me wonder if I could have gotten over Brian if it hadn't been for him. Would I have accepted Brian's offer?

I had no choice. Alana is pregnant.

Hell, no. I fell in love with the wrong man, and I dodged a bullet aimed at my heart. If our relationship would've gotten any farther, it probably would've broken me beyond repair. As they began exchanging their vows, I took a deep breath, letting it all go, and wished them a good life ahead. They deserved each other. Besides, holding emotions like anger and hatred would remind me of him. I didn't want that. When I left this venue today, I'd hold no remnants of my past relationship.

I stayed by Orlando's side as the reception began. Many people greeted him, giving me curious glances. My parents tiptoed around us. It was as if they were contemplating if they wanted to talk to us. My dad caught Orlando's eye and nodded.

Orlando dragged me to the dance floor. When his strong hands encircled my waist, the world around us faded, and it was just us. I gazed into his eyes and saw my future, wondering if he felt the same.

Life didn't work out for everyone like it had for me. Men like Orlando didn't come into everyone's life. There were women who ended their lives, women who broke down and never got up, women who still lived with scars, too afraid of another relationship. The advantage I had was I knew Orlando, and it was easy to trust him again. I believed he wouldn't leave me with a broken heart or betray my emotions.

The thing between us didn't have a status yet. We didn't know how it would turn out. But even if we did not work out as lovers, I wanted him to be a part of my life for the years to come.

With a sigh, I rested my cheek on his chest, listening to the beat of his heart. The steady rhythm calmed my nerves. It would hurt me if he walked away. The choice to remain with him was easy. I knew the risks. But it was my decision to make.

When I gazed into those gray eyes again, I knew this was just the beginning. Standing on tiptoe, I brought my lips to his, kissing him. *I'll cherish these moments while they last. And worry about the what-ifs when the time comes.*

When Orlando excused himself to use the restroom, I was left alone to wander the buffet tables.

"Thanks for coming. I thought you wouldn't show up."

I stiffened, hearing her voice, and then relaxed. My shoulders slumped when I moved to choose a dessert. "Congratulations." I didn't turn to see her yet.

"Mike brought a truck and vacated your room this morning."

"Oh."

"Are you moving in with him?"

I turned to face her, my twin. She looked beautiful as she always did. I loved her gown. Nice selection, but I would not tell her that. "Why would you ask?"

Alana looked down at her hands. "He seems like a good guy. I'm happy for you."

My brows jerked, and I tilted my head. Was she the one talking? We rarely spoke with each other, and when we did, it was to disagree about something. It wasn't the moment to start an argument. She probably looked forward to it. To make me look like a villain. "He is." I forced a smile. "Thank you."

Alana nodded and cleared her throat. "Um...Look, I'm sorry about earlier. I was just worried you'd mess with the wedding."

Did she hit her head or something?

Alana wasn't sentimental. Maybe it was the pregnancy. "Are you all right?" I asked.

"Yeah, of course." Her smile was forced, I could tell. Her gaze swept around us as if looking for someone. "So, um...I--"

"Alana, Ms. Gregory wants to talk to you."

I didn't turn to see my mom standing there. Didn't have to. I was in no mood for her judgmental glare.

"Good job, Arianna. Finally, you managed to snag yourself a rich one."

My fists clenched, and my head whipped around to meet her gaze. It was filled with disgust for reasons I wasn't aware of. What was her problem? I smiled sweetly at her. "Like you snagged Dad, right?"

Her features hardened, going from that soft, graceful look to red, hard, and murderous. "When this wedding is over, I never want to see you again."

"The feeling is mutual."

The muscle in her jaw ticked, and she opened her mouth to say something but changed her mind and stormed away.

When I turned, I saw Orlando coming my way, looking relaxed. "Shall we leave?" he asked.

The desire in his eyes warmed my heart and heated my blood. *And I'm done here.*

"Yes."

The distant sound of cheers drifted around us as we exited, bidding goodbye to the family that never wanted me. He brought my hand to his lips and kissed it before opening the car door for me.

Rain drizzled without warning, bringing the sound of distressed squeaks from the garden, and we drove toward our beginning.

Afterword

Thank you so much for reading *Getting Over Him*. I really hope you enjoyed this story. If you liked it, do consider leaving reviews. Reviews encourage the authors and help readers to discover new books.

If you'd like to stay updated on my new releases, giveaways, etc., do subscribe to my newsletter.

I'm also active on Twitter, Facebook, and Instagram. Also, you can join my Facebook group "Catherine's Book Café." I love to hear from my readers.

Have questions? Feel free to email me – catherine@catherineedward.com.

Love,

Catherine Edward

Acknowledgements

Rachelle Mills, I still remember how nervous I was when I talked to you about this plot. Your story "The Girl Who Stole My World" has helped me in a lot of ways than one. Your encouragement was everything I could ask for. I'm thankful to have you and the wonderful community of #InternationalWildflowerPack in my life.

Special thanks to author Mama Maggie--What would I have done without you, Mama? You're a wonderful person, and I feel proud to call you my soul sister. Thank you for all the motivations throughout the writing process. I love you.

Thank you Alyssa Urbano *(AerithSage)*, Jennise K, Richa Resa, Sarah Royal, Kassandra Young (K.A. Young), Ysa Archangel, E.S. Young, Sissi O. Simons, and Jo Lee Hunt for always having my back.

About the author

Catherine is passionate about Lycans, Werewolves, Witches, and Vampires, and writes sizzling tales of love and betrayal.

Her love for books started from a very young age, when her father would gift her books like Russian Tales woven with fantasy. But it was in late 2015 when she found the books of Paranormal Romance author Cynthia Eden, whose books introduced her to the whole new world of paranormal romance. The more she read, the more she got enticed, and she penned her first novel in 2016.

When she isn't writing, she likes to travel and read. Music and writing go hand in hand for this night owl. Her family and fur babies are her world.

Also by

Randolph Duology:

- Lycan's Blood Queen (Book 1)

- The Hybrid Queen (Book 2)

Moving On:

- Resisting Her

- Getting Over Him (Bonus Novella – Arianna's POV)

Phantom Agents:

- Husband Undercover (Phantom Agents Book 1)

Anthology:

- Beyond The Hallow Grave: Editingle Halloween Anthology

- Snowflakes and Winter Dreams: Editingle Winter Anthology: Vol 1

www.ingramcontent.com/pod-product-compliance
Lightning Source LLC
Chambersburg PA
CBHW022001120726
47992CB00001B/363